OUR SHARED HISTORY

The RELOCATION of NATIVE PEOPLES of NORTH AMERICA

Nicki Peter Petrikowski and Judith Edwards

Enslow Publishing
101 W. 23rd Street
Suite 240
New York, NY 10011
USA

Published in 2016 by Enslow Publishing, LLC
101 W. 23rd Street, Suite 240, New York, NY 10011

Copyright © 2016 by Judith Edwards
Enslow Publishing materials copyright © 2016 by Enslow Publishing, LLC

All rights reserved.

No part of this book may be reproduced by any means without the written permission of the publisher.

Cataloging-in-Publication Data
Petrikowski, Nicki Peter.
The relocation of native peoples of North America / by Nicki Peter Petrikowski and Judith Edwards.
p. cm. — (Our shared history)
Includes bibliographical references and index.
ISBN 978-0-7660-7012-7 (library binding)
1. Indians of North America — Relocation — Juvenile literature. 2. Indian reservations — Juvenile literature. 3. Indians of North America — Government relations — Juvenile literature.
I. Petrikowski, Nicki Peter. II. Edwards, Judith. III. Title.
E98.R4 P48 2016
323.1197—d23

Printed in the United States of America

To Our Readers: We have done our best to make sure all Web Site addresses in this book were active and appropriate when we went to press. However, the author and the publisher have no control over and assume no liability for the material available on those Web sites or any Web sites they may link to. Any comments or suggestions can be sent by e-mail to customerservice@enslow.com.

Portions of this book originally appeared in the book *The History of the American Indians and the Reservation.*

Photo Credits: Alfred Jacob Miller/WikimediaCommons/The Trapper's Bride.jpg/public domain, p. 24; Alonzo Chappel/Wikimedia Commons/ChappelWyomingMassacre.jpg/public domain, p. 25; Apic/Hulton Archive/Getty Images, p. 79; Ann Ronan Pictures/Print Collector/Hulton Archive/Getty Images, pp. 10, 55, 62, 97; © AP Images, pp. 59, 107, 117, 127, 129, 144; AP Photo/The Canadian Press, Fred Chartrand, p. 86; Buyenlarge/Archive Photos/Getty Images, pp. 12, 87; Chris Johns/National Geographic/Getty Images, p. 135; Cú Faoil/Wikimedia Commons/Custer Staghounds.jpg/public domain, p. 60; David P. Smith/Shutterstock.com, p. 142; Enno Meyer/Cincinnati Museum Center/Archive Photos/Getty Images, p. 90; Everett Historical/Shutterstock.com, p. 29; F. A. Rinehart/Buyenlarge/Getty Images, p. 1; Felix c/Wikimedia Commons/Crazy Horse 1877.jpg/public domain, p. 7; George Eastman House/Premium Archive/Getty Images, p. 8; Herbert Orth/The LIFE Images Collection/Getty Images, p. 40; ilolab/Shutterstock.com (textured background throughout book); John Mix Stanley/The Granger Collection/Wikimedia Commons/Pontiac-chief-artist-impression-414px.jpg/public domain, p. 22; John N. Choate/MPI/Archive Photo/Getty Images, p. 83; John N. Choate/Beinecke Rare Book & Manuscript Library, Yale University/Wikimedia Commons/Tom Torlino Navajo before and after circa 1882.jpg/public domain, p. 84; Keystone-France/Gamma-Keystone via Getty Images, p. 109; Library of Congress Prints and Photographs Division (chapter head photos throughout book), pp. 4, 21, 52, 68, 72, 94, 105; Lincoln Rogers/Shutterstock.com, p. 137; Mario Tama/Getty Images News/Getty Images, p. 139; Marion Post Wolcott/MPI/Archive Photos/Getty Images, p. 122; MPI/Archive Photos/Getty Images, pp. 27, 47, 66, 70, 74, 77, 88; MPI/Hulton Archive/Getty Images, p. 20; Nelson Cook, painter C. Turner, engraver/Archives of Ontario/Wikimedia Commons/Francis Bond Head.jpg, p. 44; Nikater/Demis/Wikimedia Commons/ Trail of Tears en.png/public domain, p. 35; © North Wind Picture Archives, p. 50; Photo12/UIG via Getty Images, p. 38; PhotoQuest/Archive Photos/Getty Images, p. 119; Robert Alexander/Archive Photos/Getty Images, p. 131, 133; Robfergusonjr/Courtesy Oklahoma Historical Society/Wikimedia Commons/ ChoctawCoders.jpg/public domain, p. 101; Saxton T. Pope/Wikimedia Commons/Ishi 1914.jpg/public domain, p. 103; Stock Montage/Archive Photos/Getty Images, p. 14; Transcendental Graphics/Archive Photos/Getty Images, pp. 92, 111; ullstein bild/ullstein bild via Getty Images, pp. 16, 57; Underwood Archives/Archive Photos/Getty Images, p. 113; US Army Signal Corps/National Archives and Records Administration/Wikimedia Commons/Shoshone indians.jpg/public domain, p. 42; US Department of the Interior/US Geological Survey, p. 124.

Cover Photo: Rinehart/Buyenlarge/GettyImages (Sauk Family); ilolab/Shutterstock.com(textured background).

CONTENTS

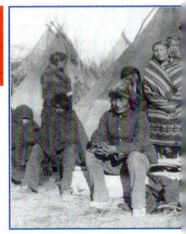

Chapter 1	Resistance Against Reservations	5
Chapter 2	The Coming of the Europeans	9
Chapter 3	The Loss of Freedom	18
Chapter 4	Supplanting the Natives	28
Chapter 5	Pushing Westward and Northward	36
Chapter 6	Armed Conflict	49
Chapter 7	Indian Suffering	64
Chapter 8	Forced Assimilation	81
Chapter 9	Buyout of Indian Land	96
Chapter 10	Steps Toward Multiculturalism	104
Chapter 11	Political Movements	115
Chapter 12	Reservations Today	130
Timeline		146
Chapter Notes		149
Glossary		155
Further Reading		156
Index		157

A young Oglala girl sits in front of a tipi near the Pine Ridge reservation around the turn of the twentieth century.

Chapter 1

Resistance Against Reservations

"Crazy Horse said to me, 'I'm glad you are come. We are going to fight the white man again.'

"The camp was already full of wounded men, women and children.

"I said to Crazy Horse, 'All right, I am ready to fight. I have fought already. My people have been killed, my horses stolen; I am satisfied to fight.'"

Two Moons (Cheyenne), recalling the events of 1876[1]

Just like other Sioux and Cheyenne leaders, Two Moons, chief of a Cheyenne Indian band, opposed the United States's 1875 order that all Sioux live only on reservations. But buffalo and other game were scarce and his people were hungry. So Two Moons had decided that he would bring his band to a reservation in southeastern Montana. The Cheyenne had formed a village near the camp of Crazy Horse, an

The RELOCATION of NATIVE PEOPLES of NORTH AMERICA

Oglala Sioux leader who resented being told to move onto a reservation. Crazy Horse was angry about broken treaties that had promised American Indians access to hunting lands in the Black Hills region of South Dakota and the Powder River and Big Horn countryside in Montana and Wyoming. Meanwhile, white settlers and miners were taking over these lands.

One dawn, in March 1876, while the Cheyenne families led by Two Moons were asleep, six companies of US Cavalry descended on the sleeping village. Quickly rising and summoning his warriors, Two Moons gathered the women and children and sent them to Crazy Horse's camp. Children were crying, their mothers were crying and comforting and hurrying, and the warriors were grabbing weapons.

Two Moons rallied his warriors and with great bravery counterattacked the cavalry. The Indians fought so fiercely that the soldiers turned their horses and galloped from the village, setting fire to tipis as they left. This attack, and the destruction of his village, angered Two Moons so much that his people camped with Crazy Horse and gave up the idea of entering a reservation.

The demand to submit to the reservation led Sitting Bull, a Hunkpapa Lakota leader whose opinion mattered to the Sioux, to remark with scorn that those who did not rebel against the reservation order and the rations it promised were "slaves to a piece of fat bacon, some hardtack [a stiff biscuit] and a little sugar and coffee."[2]

Resistance Against Reservations

Crazy Horse was the leader of the Oglala Lakota, a division of the Sioux, in the mid-1800s.

8 The RELOCATION of NATIVE PEOPLES of NORTH AMERICA

Lakota leader Sitting Bull felt that American Indians should fight against reservations because those who lived on the land got little support from the government.

Chapter 2

The Coming of the Europeans

According to anthropologist Henry A. Dobyns there could have been more than ninety million people living in North and South America in 1491, the year before the arrival of the explorer Christopher Columbus.[1] This figure of the American Indian population before the coming of the Europeans has been disputed. However, it is based on scientific studies that are increasingly respected. This could mean that in 1491 there were more people living in the Americas than in Europe. (According to a 1999 estimate from the United Nations, there were about 500 million people living on earth at the beginning of the sixteenth century. The most densely populated area was Central America.[2]) The estimates for North America vary widely, ranging from two to eighteen million people.

Columbus named these people "Indians" because he was trying to sail around the world to China and he thought he had landed in the East Indies when

The RELOCATION of NATIVE PEOPLES of NORTH AMERICA

he arrived at islands in the Caribbean Sea, south of the United States. "Most Indians view the arrival of Columbus as the beginning of a four-hundred-year cycle of disease, exploitation, enslavement and genocide that devastated them as a race of people," says historian George Russell, who is a Saginaw Chippewa Indian.[3] A Canadian census in 1871 gave the number of that country's Aboriginal, or native, population as 102,358,[4] while the official US Census Bureau count in 1900 gave the number of Indians living in the United States as 237,196.[5] Over the course of a few centuries contact with the new settlers had reduced the native population to a fraction of what it once was.

Columbus presented gifts to the first natives to greet him on his landing in America.

The Coming of the Europeans

Origin of America's Aboriginal People

Where did the Indians of America come from? And when did they arrive? Ideas vary, but the most widely accepted theory is that they migrated from Asia across the Bering Strait, using a land bridge from Siberia to Alaska, which was above water during the last ice age. Even today it is possible to cross the Bering Strait on foot when it is frozen, although it is extremely dangerous.

The experts are divided over when the migration to present-day Alaska occurred—estimates range from fifty thousand years ago to a mere twelve thousand years ago—and whether it happened in a single wave or in multiple stages. Even though the exact details are unclear, the Bering Strait theory is generally considered more plausible than competing ideas that the ancestors of America's Aboriginal people could have arrived via water travel or might have evolved independently from the rest of humanity.

Arising Conflict

In the early 1700s, Europeans were beginning to settle in the New World. In some cases, American Indians greeted the settlers who came to their land with generosity. They agreed to the settlers' occupying specific pieces of land. The Pilgrim colony at Plymouth, Massachusetts, learned how to survive in this new world because of the skills their Wampanaog neighbors shared with them. But when more people arrived who needed more land, it was just taken. Then conflict arose.

12 The RELOCATION of NATIVE PEOPLES of NORTH AMERICA

This map shows where different American Indian nations lived before the arrival of European settlers, around 1492.

The Coming of the Europeans

"From then on the Indian was in almost constant retreat before the stream of pioneers heading westward, where demand for land never ceased," says historian Ralph Andrist.[6]

However, long before the colonies at Jamestown and Plymouth were even thought of, European expeditions had changed the lives of the American Indians. There were once about five hundred Indian groups in what is now the United States, all speaking different languages.[7]

Popular stories and films show all American Indians living on the plains, riding horses, and living in tipis. They wear war paint and feathers. American Indians at the first Thanksgiving are shown sharing harvest food with the Pilgrims. The reality of American Indians is a much more diverse and complex picture.

In the southeastern part of North America, the American Indian grouping is called the Mississippian Culture, or the Mississippi Mound Civilization. This was not the nomadic culture of the Great Plains, but a people who were well-organized in seasonal farming communities. Tragically, contact in 1539 with an early Spanish explorer, Hernando de Soto, left this culture devastated from battle and disease.

By the mid-seventeenth century, when the English and French reached inland southeastern North America, the remaining Mississippian people had scattered. Their culture evolved into different American Indian groups. The remaining bands of Mississippian Indians, disorganized and completely without their old stable social, religious, and family

14 The RELOCATION of NATIVE PEOPLES of NORTH AMERICA

An Algonquian village of 1590 North Carolina is depicted in this engraving. Cornfields can be seen at the right, and American Indians prepare food in the center of the picture.

The Coming of the Europeans

structure, became the Creek, Muskogee, Choctaw, Chickasaw, and Cherokee nations.

In the Northeast, the Algonquian-speaking peoples lived in present-day New York and Ohio. The Iroquoians lived on lands that included the interior waterways, especially around the Great Lakes. Six Iroquoian tribes—the Mohawk, Onondaga, Seneca, Oneida, Cayuga, and later, the Tuscarora—formed a group called the League of the Longhouse.

Again, an expedition of Europeans changed the destiny of this powerful nation. Around 1550, during Jacques Cartier's exploration of the St. Lawrence River in what is now Quebec, Canada, European trade goods were introduced to the Iroquois. Iron tools, which reduced the amount of time needed to cut or scrape animal parts and hides, became particularly prized possessions. So did such items as beads, cloth, and mirrors, because they became status symbols. By the time the Dutch arrived in 1614 to build Fort Nassau near Albany, New York, the League's access and dependence on European goods was a fact of life. This affected not only the Iroquois, but the powerful Huron who lived in the territory north and west of the Iroquois and Algonquian territories. The Huron maintained a powerful and complex trade network. Their nation was weakened by European disease, leaving them vulnerable to attack and social problems.

This unraveling of the American Indian world was going on simultaneously through all the land that would become the original thirteen colonies. The generosity with which the Wampanoag had greeted

16   The RELOCATION of NATIVE PEOPLES of NORTH AMERICA

Jacques Cartier meets with Canadian Indians for the first time.

the new colonists at Plymouth was not returned. By 1633, the expanding Pilgrim colony had used all available land and found excuses to invade lands belonging to the surviving bands of Wampanoag.

Clashing Ways of Living

All the Algonquian speakers, whether hunters or farmers, knew that corn had a 160-day growing season. In the fall, after the corn had ripened, American Indian villages disbanded. Indians traveled with the seasons and the availability of game. They had no concept of individual land ownership. To them, land and sea and water were similar elements, and how could a person own any of those?

The Indians combined farming, gathering, hunting, and fishing. The colonists, who lived in permanent

The Coming of the Europeans

houses much more cramped and unhealthy than the Indian dwellings, had no understanding of the Indian "way of the land." They saw only that for part of a year land was unused, which made them think they had the right to take it over.

Dangers of New Diseases

Diseases such as smallpox, cholera, and the flu killed more of the American Indian population over the years than armed conflict. Indians had no immunity to the diseases that were brought over by Europeans. Many American Indians were wiped out by disease—particularly smallpox. Struggling survivors were sometimes sold into slavery to work on plantations. These raids disrupted the agricultural cycle. People were afraid to go out hunting because of the raiders.

Weakened by a lack of food, the people were all the more susceptible to diseases to which most white men had built up immunity for over many centuries, resulting in a vicious circle that led to the death of many American Indians.

Chapter 3

The Loss of Freedom

The number of Europeans living in the colonies in the New World grew quickly, and by 1671, there were already fifty thousand settlers in the area that would become the United States.[1] Though earlier settlers traded with and learned from the American Indians, the hunger for land changed that relationship. The European settlers labeled the Indians as uncivilized, even savage. They took over lands used by the Indians. Bounties (rewards of money) were sometimes placed on the scalps of Indian men, women, and children.

Ill-Fated Alliances

The area near the eastern part of the border of what became Canada and the United States was the territory of the Iroquois. The Iroquois were also known as the Five Nations, made up of the Mohawk, Onondaga, Cayuga, and Seneca nations. They were powerful allies of the British. The French were aligned with the Algonquin and Huron, enemies of the Five Nations,

The Loss of Freedom

and had set up a string of trading posts for receiving valuable beaver pelts and dispensing European goods to the Indians. This was to lead to terrible consequences for the Indians, because they became more dependent on European goods, especially tools. Manufactured items always exceeded the value of what Indians could trade, so the balance of trade was unequal. American Indian lands were overhunted, depleting the game that supplied food and clothing. This led to the need to trap in areas used by other Indians, which led to warfare. The Huron, formerly the mightiest tribe in what is now Eastern Canada, lost more than two thirds of their number to epidemics and were almost wiped out by the Mohawk, the northernmost tribe of the Iroquois Confederacy, in the middle seventeenth century. Indians were coerced into selling land through treaties, which were hard for them to understand.

However, the French and the Iroquois coexisted as two sovereign nations—for a time that is. In general, the contact between the French settlers and the Natives seems to have been more peaceful and cooperative than can be said for the English or the Spanish, although the reasons for that are the specific circumstances rather than humanitarian philosophy. The French were fewer in number in the New World than the other European powers, and they were more dependent on the help of the Aboriginal people. They also were less intent on taking the Natives' land than their European rivals operating further south.[2]

The RELOCATION of NATIVE PEOPLES of NORTH AMERICA

A sketch depicts French settlers, led by Samuel de Champlain, launching a surprise attack on an Iroquois camp during the French and Indian War.

Nevertheless, from 1754 to 1763, the Iroquois joined the British in fighting the French and their Indian allies. This became known as the French and Indian War. Historian Richard White writes: "In hindsight the possibilities for Indian independence within the mixed political world of the mid-eighteenth century began to change in 1763 when England defeated France in the [French and Indian War.]"[3]

"The world of mutual dependence and accommodation, in which the Indians and the whites could find a place for one another, was disappearing," according to historian Landon Jones.[4]

The Loss of Freedom

Forceful Expansion

Lord Jeffrey Amherst, the British army commander in North America, believed that after the war the American Indians were subjects of the British Crown. They had no choice but to do what Britain dictated.[5] The Delaware, Shawnee, and Ottawa nations, who had already been driven from their homelands in the East, rebelled against the British repression and against rival American Indians.

Amherst's actions led to what is known as "Pontiac's Rebellion," though in fact Pontiac was just one of several Ottawa chiefs. Pontiac, joined by other powerful chiefs, led a rebellion against the British. When the Indians were told they were subjects of a British king they knew was not their leader, it tipped the scales in

American Indians, along with French forces, defeated the British at this battle in Virginia in 1755.

22 The RELOCATION of NATIVE PEOPLES of NORTH AMERICA

Chief Pontiac led his people in fighting the British.

favor of violence. Lord Amherst suggested that blankets contaminated with smallpox be sent to the tribes involved in the rebellion.

"The commander of Fort Pitt invited some of the besieging Delawares to a parley, and gave the small-pox-infected blankets from the fort hospital as a token of esteem. As the ensuing epidemic raged it progressively undermined the Indians' ability to fight,

The Loss of Freedom

and the tide of war quickly turned against them," says historian James Wilson.[6]

Before the American Revolution, the British had set the Appalachian Mountains as the western border for their colonies. The Royal Proclamation, issued by King George III in 1763, was intended to integrate the land formerly held by the French into the British Empire. The proclamation forbade white settlers from establishing homes beyond the mountains. This act confirmed the boundary already established in the 1744 Treaty of Lancaster. In addition to accepting that the natives had an inherent right to the land they lived on, the Royal Proclamation also determined that settlers were no longer allowed to buy land from the Indians, instead only allowing the Crown to buy land from the natives. Unfortunately, the pressures for more land for more people made this treaty invalid almost before it was written. There were simply not enough army officers and local laws to keep colonists from moving west past the mountains.

"The British authorities . . . unable to enforce their laws, . . . decided to rewrite them. Unable to protect Indian lands, they took them," says historian Landon Jones.[7]

Independence Won and Lost

In the aftermath of the Revolutionary War, in which the American colonists defeated Great Britain and formed the United States of America, the victorious Americans claimed that the Indians were also conquered and had to give up their lands as a consequence. Some who had

The RELOCATION of NATIVE PEOPLES of NORTH AMERICA

Cultural Blend

Indians not only taught European settlers about new crops, such as corn and squash, they also helped the settlers hunt and live in the wild new land. Intermarriage between white frontiersmen and American Indian women was common, encouraged even in case of the French fur traders operating in the Great Lakes region in the eighteenth century as close ties with the natives benefitted their trade. Such unions were the origin of the Métis, whose mixed European and Native American ancestry has produced a unique way of life. Today the Métis are one of the three recognized Aboriginal peoples of Canada, although it took until 2003 for Canada to give the Métis the same rights as the Indian peoples of the First Nations, another group of Aborigines.

A European settler weds a young American Indian.

The Loss of Freedom

American Indian and British soldiers defeated American colonists at the Battle of Wyoming in Pennsylvania on July 3, 1778.

fought alongside the British, particularly the members of the Iroquois Confederacy, fled north, where the British Crown established two reserves for the Six Nations (the Tuscarora had joined the Five Nations of the Mohawk, Onondaga, Oneida, Cayuga, and Seneca) on land surrendered by the Odawa, Ojibwa and Algonquin living around the Great Lakes.

The Treaty of Greenville, signed in 1795, gave major land grants to the Americans in exchange for payment and goods. The American Indians gave up a large portion of what is now Ohio, as well as other areas. In return, the United States agreed that land north and west of the treaty line would belong to the Indians. "The treaty signed at Greenville was the most

The RELOCATION of NATIVE PEOPLES of NORTH AMERICA

important Indian treaty in the nation's history," says historian Landon Jones.[8]

The treaty and its aftermath set the stage for negotiations between American Indians and the US government from then on. First, whites occupied Indian lands. The Indians would retaliate by raids on the settlements. The settlers would demand military protection. The military and the Indians would engage in battles and raids. Often starved out by having their crops destroyed and no longer having land on which to hunt or grow crops, the Indians would surrender. This surrender always meant they were coerced into giving away even more of their land.

A sort of peace reigned in the area until two Shawnee brothers, Tecumseh and Tenskawatawa, tried to rally the scattered American Indians into an alliance they hoped would lead to peace. Fighting broke out nonetheless. As the War of 1812 led to more betrayals, fighting gradually ceased. Many Indians who had sided with the British in the war decided to move north to Upper Canada.

Contact with the Europeans had caused the Indian population to decrease [dramatically in number, more due to disease than armed conflict. The future looked bleak for the rest of the American Indians.

The Loss of Freedom

Tecumseh and his people, the Shawnee, tried to form an alliance with other American Indians.

Chapter 4

Supplanting the Natives

The idea of a land exchange, which would mean removing the American Indians east of the Mississippi River, had been suggested by President Thomas Jefferson as early as 1802. He realized that it was going to be impossible to protect the Indians from having their land seized by state expansion. Treaty violations continued as more settlers wanted more land.

The US Congress did not accept the idea of removal and land exchange at that time. The Louisiana Purchase (1803), and the opening of the west through the Lewis and Clark Expedition (1804–1806), created a vast new area for expansion. After the end of the War of 1812, the idea of a land exchange was again considered. By then, the boundary had been pushed farther west than the Appalachian Mountains. A permanent territory between the Mississippi River and the Rocky Mountains was now considered the "ideal solution" to the Indian problem.[1]

Supplanting the Natives

The expedition of Lewis and Clark, shown here in a painting by Frederic Remington, allowed Americans to stake their claim on new territories. As a result, the American Indians were pushed even further west.

Problematic Coexistence

In 1824 a bill signed by Secretary of War John C. Calhoun created a Bureau of Indian Affairs. The first superintendent of the bureau, Thomas L. McKenney, realized that removal was the only policy that northeastern settlers would tolerate. He made statements that indicated that if Indians were not removed from the northeast, they would quickly face extinction.[2]

The Permanent Indian Territory that had opened up west of the Alleghenies and especially in the territory of the Louisiana Purchase, had a major complication. It happened to be the homeland of many other American Indian nations who had always

The RELOCATION of NATIVE PEOPLES of NORTH AMERICA

lived in the west. What was to be done with these other Indians? And, what problems would it cause for the unwilling intruders, such as the Cherokee, to be seen as invading someone else's territory?

This had crossed the minds of the settlers familiar with the Indians along the Missouri River, who were having their own difficulties living near the existing American Indians. During the first few years of American independence, the new government made peace treaties with American Indians in outlying areas. These peace treaties were always written in ways that ensured large chunks of land would go to the white settlers. However, there was still an option for large Indian nations, such as the Delaware of the northeast coast, or the Cherokee in the southeast, to either join the union as a state or to remain a sovereign nation.

The Cherokee and related nations in the South realized, after the American Revolution, that further resistance to the white invaders was impossible. Most of the tribes—even the powerful Muskogee, also called the Creek—tried to create governments that were similar to the newly created American republic. The Cherokee used the American example to set up a constitution as a sovereign nation. The colonists in the state of Georgia, despite the Cherokee's decision to never again sell any of their land, simply declared their constitution invalid. Georgia then divided up the Cherokee's land into separate counties of the state.

The Cherokee were saddened and angered by the realization that no matter what they did or how well they succeeded in living the same as the white settlers,

Supplanting the Natives

> ## Legal Action
>
> The Cherokee went to the new United States Supreme Court to object to the takeover of their land. In a famous court case, called *Cherokee Nation* v. *State of Georgia*, 1831, the court ruled that yes, the Cherokee and other American Indian groups were foreign nations, but since they occupied land in the United States they were actually "domestic dependents" and the court therefore felt it was not able to rule in the case.

they would always be viewed as inferior. They had hoped that treaty obligations would protect them, but the constant hunger for land from increasing numbers of settlers signaled the final stage of the American Indian removal policy: reservations.

Transport to the First Reservations

The first reservations were simply areas of land called territories, to which American Indians were transported. The term "Trail of Tears" specifically refers to the 1838 march of fifteen thousand Cherokee during which four thousand people died from starvation, disease, and brutal weather conditions.[3] However, the larger Trail of Tears was the actual Indian Removal

The RELOCATION of NATIVE PEOPLES of NORTH AMERICA

Act of 1830, which led to ten years of brutal marches. During this time about sixty thousand individuals from Cherokee, Chickasaw, Choctaw, Creek, and Seminole nations were removed from their southeastern homes and sent to the Indian Territory.[4] This number becomes higher when other relocations, totaling some sixty Indian groups, are included.[5]

This territory set aside for relocation was defined as being west of the Mississippi and not in the states of Missouri, Louisiana, or the territory of Arkansas. President Andrew Jackson signed the Indian Removal Act in violation of a US Supreme Court case (*Worcester v. Georgia*) under Chief Justice John Marshall, which held that state laws could not be enforced on American Indian lands. When informed of this legal decision, Jackson replied, "John Marshall has made his decision. Now let him enforce it!"[6]

In the area around St. Louis, Missouri, nations such as the Osage and the Kansas had to be dealt with before full-scale removal could take place. William Clark, Superintendent of Indian Affairs, was charged with handling the Indians who might be in the way of eastern tribes emigrating west. William Clark noted in his logbook, during September 1826, that members of the Shawnee, Potawatomi, Kickapoo, Delaware, Osage, and Peoria nations applied to him for provisions to move west.[7]

By the end of 1827, it was hard to keep up with the needs for food and clothing for the large numbers of Indians whose lands had been confiscated and who had no way to make a living. "The tribes on this side

Supplanting the Natives

New Land, New Problems

The Cherokee and other tribes who did make it alive to Indian Territory were only beginning their hardship. Basically farmers, they had trouble growing enough food on land that had never before been plowed and was often not suitable. The government did not send the equipment and seeds they had promised. Other nations, such as the Comanche, Kiowa, and Pawnee, who were already there, were hunters whose major food source was the buffalo. They resented this invasion into their territory. Nations who had cooperated in the past became rivals.

of the Mississippi are wretched and moving from place to place . . . the distresses of the Indians of this Superintendency are so great and extensive, and complaints so frequent, it is, and has been impossible for me to report them. I therefore have taken upon myself a great deal, in acting as I thought best."[8] Clark was not the only American who was outraged by the treatment of the Indians—though he seems to have shared the

The RELOCATION of NATIVE PEOPLES of NORTH AMERICA

majority opinion that removal was the only way to save them from extinction.

Before this increasing number of American Indians moving west could even get started on the trail, smallpox again struck their people. Reports were that at least half of the people in the nations on the lower Missouri had died. But in Washington, the War Department was more interested in reports on the fur trade than on this tragedy.

The unwilling immigrants to the plains area designated as Indian Territory, which was also labeled The Great American Desert or Permanent Indian Country, tried valiantly to start their lives anew. The Indian Appropriations Act of 1851 formed official reservations from the territories occupied by the dislodged eastern nations. Already reservations had been set aside in the south and northwest.

Soon, powerful forces, including gold strikes in the formerly Spanish-held southwest and California, and farther north in Oregon territory, would again take homes away from this devastated culture. Perhaps if it had not been for the gold strikes in California, the huge surge of migration to what had appeared to be desert and mountainous country too difficult to cross would not have happened. But due to the gold rush, one hundred and seventy-five thousand headed west between 1849 and 1852 to seek their fortune, and on their way they had to cross Indian Territory.[9]

Supplanting the Natives

This map shows the route of the Trail of Tears for relocation of Native Americans from the Southeastern United States between 1836 and 1839.

Chapter 5

Pushing Westward and Northward

After gold was discovered in California in 1848, miners, settlers, and the eastern American Indians already removed to the western territories flocked to the lands that promised wealth. However, even before the huge migration caused by the gold rush, Indians in what are now the northwestern and southwestern United States were affected. Indians along the Santa Fe trade routes were becoming aggressive as their homelands were invaded and game became scarce. In the Rocky Mountains, the constant hunting for furs had depleted game. Between 1800 and 1840, three smallpox pandemics had devastating effects on many of the Plains Indians. An effort had been made in 1832 to inoculate the Western Indian tribes against the repeated outbreaks of smallpox. Unfortunately, the efforts stopped before the doctors reached the Mandan, the Arikara, the Assiniboine, and the Cree.

Pushing Westward and Northward

With the Settlers Came the Disease

Steamboats had been going up and down the Missouri River since 1818. In 1837 a steamboat called the *St. Peters* carried a passenger who came down with smallpox. The ensuing epidemic killed many members of the nations that had been visited by the Lewis and Clark expedition. The Mandan Indians, whose nation was already affected by smallpox, numbered about sixteen hundred in early 1837. By the end of that year, there were only thirty-one Mandan left. More than half of the Arikara Indians died. The Cree, with about three thousand tribal members, and the Assiniboines, who had numbered ten thousand, were almost completely wiped out.[1] The Blackfeet in the Rocky Mountains were the next to be affected. Only the Lakota Sioux, off on a buffalo hunt in the far reaches of their territory, came out of this particular epidemic with little harm.[2]

Bureau of Indian Affairs agent Joshua Pilcher wrote to William Clark that "The country through which [the smallpox epidemic] has passed is literally depopulated and converted into one great graveyard."[3] In an effort to find the Lakota Sioux and inoculate them, Clark and Pilcher hired a doctor, Joseph R. De Prefontaine, to give vaccinations. About three thousand Indians were vaccinated as the steamboat stopped along the Missouri River. The Lakota Sioux were never reached, due to the doctor's own illness.

38 The RELOCATION of NATIVE PEOPLES of NORTH AMERICA

Steamboats carried settlers to new territories. Along with the settlers came diseases that devastated many Indian groups.

Fighting for Territory

By 1850 the United States had managed to rid itself of all European territorial claims from the Atlantic Ocean to the Pacific Ocean. The only obstacle to complete settlement of the West were the American Indian nations, many of whom had been already reduced by disease, alcohol, and hunger. Because of the large numbers of people migrating through their territory, the Plains Indians became the next to be affected by settlers moving west.

The Plains Indians, with the possible exception of the Blackfeet confederacy, did not have the unity of the Iroquois nations. The Plains Indians had become swift riders after European explorers introduced them to horses. Hunting game, especially buffalo, was a way of life, and highly territorial. As the game disappeared,

Pushing Westward and Northward

Demise in California

The native groups of California may have suffered the greatest losses when their land, once belonging to Mexico, was won by the United States. Eighteen Indian groups were talked into signing treaties for reservations, but there were so many objections from white settlers at giving Indians any land that could possibly be used for agriculture and mining that the treatgies were never honored. Instead, the government rewarded "volunteer armies" who wiped out entire Indian villages, so that by 1853 there was no land that belonged to Indians. After the Gold Rush, nations that had numbered four thousand to fourteen thousand had only a few, struggling survivors.[4]

Plains Indians were forced to move farther from their homes to hunt. This encroachment strained relations between nations and led to warfare.

Throughout the 1830s and 1840s, the Cheyenne and Arapaho fought the Comanche and the Kiowa; the Sioux and the Northern Cheyenne were at war with the Crow. All of these nations threatened the Shoshone and the Pawnee. The Delaware, Shawnee, Potawatomi, and other smaller nations, who had

The RELOCATION of NATIVE PEOPLES of NORTH AMERICA

been removed to Indian Territory, fought for their own space on the plains. Into this warfare came white settlers, hungry for their own land.

Some Indian groups formed war parties to attack settlers' wagon trains. Raiding parties stole cows and horses from the settlers, and the government stepped in. Of the fifty-six military posts in the United States in 1845, twenty-four of them were west of the Mississippi. In 1849 two forts were set up along the Laramie River in Wyoming, and two years later a great council of the northern nations was held at nearby Horse Creek. The number of Indians who attended this council is estimated to be ten thousand.[5]

A painting depicts a Sioux camp on the upper Missouri River. The Sioux were one of the groups of Plains Indians.

Pushing Westward and Northward

Reservations and Reserves

The word "reservation" has more than one meaning. *Webster's New World Dictionary*'s second definition is "a public land set aside for some special use."[6] *The Oxford Compact English Dictionary* is even more specific: "an area of land set aside for occupation by North American Indians or Australian Aboriginals."[7]

In Canada, the word "reserve" is used instead, which is defined in the Indian Act as "a tract of land, the legal title to which is vested in Her Majesty, that has been set apart by Her Majesty for the use and benefit of a band."[8] The fact that the land is held by the monarch rather than the bands using it complicates matters of individually-owned housing, and it is a concern to some that the control of the legal title is out of the inhabitants' hands.

42 The RELOCATION of NATIVE PEOPLES of NORTH AMERICA

Fort Washakie in Wyoming was a military post on a Shoshone and Arapaho reservation. Here Shoshones are dancing as the soldiers look on.

Nations who had never met each other except in war camped together at Horse Creek and agreed to a general peace. Assiniboine, Atsina, Arikara, Crow, Shoshone, Sioux, Cheyenne, and Arapaho agreed not to attack the wagon trains that surged through their land. In exchange, the United States promised to use its troops to protect the Indians from whites, who stole their land and attacked their villages. Two years later, in 1853, the United States made the same promises to the Comanche, Kiowa, and other southern Plains Indians. As settlers spilled across the plains, the promises fell away. The troops began a series of Indian

Pushing Westward and Northward

wars, attacking the same nations they had promised to protect.

Legalized Displacement

As the number of settlers in Canada grew during the first half of the nineteenth century, so did the hunger for land. After a number of land surrender treaties there were only some pockets of land still in the hands of the natives in Upper Canada. Many Aboriginals had lost access to their hunting grounds, and attempts to turn them into farmers were not successful.

In 1836 the Lieutenant-Governor of Upper Canada, Sir Francis Bond Head, wanted to separate the Aboriginals from the white population. To allow them to keep their traditional lifestyle and to protect them from harmful influences like alcohol, he concluded a treaty that established Manitoulin Island and nearby smaller islands in Lake Huron as a reserve. Few native groups could be convinced to move to Manitoulin Island, though. Instead, most continued to live on small areas set aside by the treaties, while the Crown continued to acquire territories as the white settlers were spreading out northwards. In the Robinson-Huron and the Robinson-Superior treaties of 1850 the Anishinaabeg peoples living around Lake Huron and Lake Superior gave up lands, where mines were to be established, in exchange for the creation of reserves, money, and the continued right to hunt and fish on these lands.[6]

The United States Congress passed the Indian Appropriations Act in 1854. This legalized the

The RELOCATION of NATIVE PEOPLES of NORTH AMERICA

formation of Indian reservations and the removal of designated tribes to specific locations. Not only the Plains Indians were affected; the Pueblo, Navajo, Ute, and Apache were removed to reservations. In Texas, the native Apache, Kiowa, and Comanche were relocated to two small reservations.

In the Northwest, the Yakima signed a treaty giving away ten million acres of their land for the promise of government supplies and support. Not all their chiefs agreed to this and battles raged for three years. However, after fighting valiantly to save their land, the remaining Yakima were confined to a small reservation in the eastern part of the state. The Blackfeet also signed a treaty that reduced their territory. In all, fifty-two treaties, which forced western Indians to live on a small amount of their former territory, were in place by 1856.

Repeated Relocation

Those Cherokee who survived the Trail of Tears and the first difficult years in a harsh land had prospered. The more they succeeded with housing, agriculture, and self-governance, the more settlers wanted the land on which they lived. Because the Cherokee and other relocated nations had retained their belief that all their citizens had a right to land—which was held by each nation and not by individuals—the entire population prospered. This only fueled the desire of land speculators to take over the land on which the Cherokee had done so well. "In the presidential election campaign of 1860, William Seward publicly declared that: "'Indian

Pushing Westward and Northward

Sir Francis Bond Head

The RELOCATION of NATIVE PEOPLES of NORTH AMERICA

Inuit

Inuit, the Aboriginal people living in the arctic and subarctic region of northern Canada, Alaska, and Greenland, came into contact with Europeans early. There is evidence that they encountered the Vikings who had come to Greenland and Canada centuries before Columbus's discovery. Later they had regular contact with fishermen, whalers, and fur traders, who left their mark on Inuit society. Trade goods became available, and the availability of wild game dwindled.

Same as the Aboriginal peoples living to the south, many Inuit died because of the diseases carried by Europeans. For a long time, though, unlike the other natives, they did not have to worry about anybody trying to take their land, which was too inhospitable for settlers. It wasn't until the mid-twentieth century that the establishment of military bases during the Cold War with Russia and the extraction of natural resources had a big impact on the living environment of the Inuit.

Pushing Westward and Northward

Territory south of Kansas must be vacated by the Indian,'" says historian James Wilson.[10]

Without the Civil War, perhaps the Cherokee might have been able to keep this land and become an example for other confined tribes. However, the unity of their government collapsed after both the Union and the Confederacy offered empty promises.

The Cherokee were not the only nation adversely affected by the Civil War, which began in 1861. In the early months of the war, the US government withdrew almost all its troops from the Plains. This meant that there were fewer American Indian attacks on wagon trains, "suggesting that, left to themselves, the supposedly bloodthirsty Sioux and other tribes were prepared to co-exist peacefully . . . and were more interested in hunting than in killing Americans," says Wilson.[11]

More than 100,000 hopeful settlers rushed onto the Cherokee Strip in Oklahoma on the day that it was opened to colonization after the removal of all Native Americans.

The RELOCATION of NATIVE PEOPLES of NORTH AMERICA

Hunger

This small reprieve was not to last. By 1862 Indians in the Northwest, having had their land and their game taken away, were suffering from hunger. The annuity payments to the Indians, which paid for the meager supplies handed out to the reservation Indians, had been reallocated to the war effort. For the Santee Sioux, who had given up nine-tenths of their territory so they could feed their people (and settlers were already encroaching on the small area they had left), it was the last straw. Bureau of Indian Affairs agent, Thomas Galbraith, refused to distribute the food without the annuity money. Gathering at the agency, the Santee chief, Ta-oya-te-duta (Little Crow), gave this speech:

> We have waited a long time. The money is ours, but we cannot get it. We have no food, but here are these stores, filled with food. We ask that you, the agent, make some arrangement by which we can get food from the stores, or else we may take our own way to keep ourselves from starving. When men are hungry they help themselves.[12]

Shortly after this, the Santee revolted, attacking the agency and settlers. The US government, despite waging a war on the Confederacy, sent soldiers and volunteer frontiersmen to fight the Indians. The resulting Indian Wars are the backdrop of today's romanticized concept of "The Wild West," but the movies don't tell the true story.

Chapter 6

Armed Conflict

"This war did not spring up here in our land; this war was brought upon us by the children of the Great Father who came to take our land from us without price, and who, in our land do a great many evil things."

Sinte-Galeshka (Spotted Tail), chief of the Brulé Lakota[1]

With more than a thousand armed conflicts between American Indians and whites in the Plains region, the years between 1860 and 1891 were a time of bloody battles in which the Indian population fought valiantly to retain their land, customs, and very existence. Already destroyed by disease and alcoholism, hungry and cold, the Plains Indian leaders fought the inevitable end of their civilization. Railroads crossed their former hunting grounds as train passengers even leaned out of windows to shoot at the diminishing herds of buffalo.

The RELOCATION of NATIVE PEOPLES of NORTH AMERICA

In the Southwest, the Navajo and Apache raided settlements not so much for food as to rescue their women and children who had been enslaved. "It was officially estimated that 2,000 Indian slaves were held by the white people of New Mexico and Arizona in 1866," says historian William Brandon.[2] This was a particular problem for the Apache, whose famous chiefs Cochise and Mangas Coloradas managed in 1861 to temporarily rid Arizona of most of its white people.

Reservations of the Mescaleros and Navajo

The Apache, also called the Mescaleros, were the first to be sent to an arid, desert reservation at Bosque Redondo, in the Pecos River Valley. Indian fighter Kit Carson, boasting that "wild Indians could be tamed,"[3] conquered the Navajo by entering Canyon de Chelly, where they lived and farmed. His troops burned their

The Cheyenne meet with white settlers.

Armed Conflict

hogans (houses), orchards, and fields, and seized their livestock. The Navajo, starving and bewildered, were driven on the "Long Walk" to Bosque Redondo. Many died of disease and starvation in that dry and desolate landscape. Four years later, the Navajo were allowed to return to a portion of their former land. They were given thirty-five thousand sheep and goats to promote sheepherding. This began a cycle of industriousness and adaptation to life. Their excellent weaving and silver jewelry-making would become a moderate success story in the future.

Chief Joseph's Resistance

The Nez Perce were superb horsemen who brought many warriors to a treaty council at Walla Walla, Washington, in 1855. There they agreed to a reduction in their territory that became the Nez Perce reservation. However, by 1860, when gold was discovered in Oregon, settlers overwhelmed the Wallowa Valley which was at the center of the Nez Perce reservation. Led by a chief called Old Joseph, the Nez Perce became known for a policy of passive resistance. They stayed on their land despite the abuses of their white "neighbors."

In 1873 the US government proclaimed the Wallowa Valley a reservation—for the second time. It had been proclaimed by a treaty already but this did not stop the settlers from murdering American Indians whenever they could. Three years later, in one more stunning reversal of a promise, the Nez Perce were told they had thirty days to move their people

52 The RELOCATION of NATIVE PEOPLES of NORTH AMERICA

Chief Joseph led the Nez Perce in a fight against US troops.

Armed Conflict

to Idaho. To not comply would be an act of war. By this time, Old Joseph had died and Young Joseph was the chief. He and a chief named Ollokut tried to negotiate peace terms while hiding their people. Finally, carrying a flag of truce, a group of US soldiers fired into a group of Nez Perce, who returned fire.

Chief Joseph marched his people seventeen hundred miles, winning skirmishes with the army repeatedly. He insisted that no killing would happen that was not defensive. Most of the other chiefs died along the way, and many of the Nez Perce starved as winter arrived. Just thirty miles from the safety of the Canadian border, Chief Joseph was forced to surrender. He and others of his tribe who refused to give up their beliefs spent the rest of their lives on the Colville reservation in Washington State's most dry region.

Massacres

The massive migration to the Western states by white settlers continued. Military pursuit to subdue the outraged Indians cost the government millions of dollars and many dead soldiers. Most of the battles during this period occurred because Indians who had been confined to a reservation on a small portion of their former land refused to stay there. They were starving—at least if they left the reservation they might be able to hunt the now scarce animals. And the reservation boundaries kept changing as white settlers found even those lands desirable.

The RELOCATION of NATIVE PEOPLES of NORTH AMERICA

Chief Joseph's Surrender

Chief Joseph's words as he surrendered have become famous as the speech of an extraordinary human being:

> I am tired of fighting. Our chiefs are killed . . . The old men are all dead. It is cold and we have no blankets. The little children are freezing to death. My people, some of them, have run away to the hills, and have no blankets, no food; no one knows where they are—perhaps freezing to death. I want to have time to look for my children and see how many I can find. Maybe I shall find them among the dead. Hear me, my chiefs. I am tired; my heart is sick and sad. From where the sun now stands I will fight no more forever.[4]

Armed Conflict

55

An illustration shows the death of Chief Joseph of the Nez-Perce in 1904.

The RELOCATION of NATIVE PEOPLES of NORTH AMERICA

The Lakota Sioux, led by Chief Red Cloud, not only defeated the army on many occasions, but attacked the various forts along the Bozeman trail. Staggering under the expense of these wars, the government signed yet another treaty at Fort Laramie in 1868, and agreed to close the Bozeman trail and leave western South Dakota as unconquered Indian territory.

This Indian victory had little impact on the poor treatment of American Indians. In 1871 the American government simply decided to stop making treaties. There would be no more treating the Indians as independent nations, but instead the goal was to get them onto reservations as quickly as possible. There they would be completely dependent on government support and rations, and perhaps could be educated.

One of the voices for making Indians wards of the government and for treating them fairly on the reservations was the Commissioner of Indian Affairs, Ely S. Parker. He was a Seneca Indian who had risen to power during the administration of President Ulysses S. Grant. Highly intelligent and motivated to succeed, Parker received his law degree and then a degree in civil engineering. He faced much discrimination when he tried to use his knowledge and skills to make a place for himself in white society, but he believed that there was no choice for Indians but to become educated in the white man's ways of life.[5]

This view of what should now be done with the Indians who were rapidly losing their lands, was at odds with other views that called for extermination.

Armed Conflict

Chief Red Cloud led a series of attacks against American forts.

The RELOCATION of NATIVE PEOPLES of NORTH AMERICA

Colonel John Gibbon won a gold medal for an essay in an Army competition, writing:

> Philanthropists and visionary speculators may theorize as they please about protecting the Indian . . . and preserving him as a race. It cannot be done. Whenever the two come in contact . . . the weaker must give way, and disappear. To deny this is to deny the evidence of our own senses, and to shut our eyes to the facts of history.[6]

Opposed to this view were those who had been outraged by the reports of the Sand Creek Massacre, in 1864. The Cheyenne Indians, "after living on government rations at Fort Lyon for a while . . . were instructed to shift their camp to Sand Creek, some thirty miles [forty-eight kilometers] from the military post, where they could hunt for themselves," says historian Peter Nabokov.[7] Instead, the Cheyenne, as well as the Arapaho camped with them, became the hunted. Seven hundred troops, in early dawn, fired on the sleeping camp and killed all they could find, "babies and mothers, warriors and grandparents."[8] Chief Black Kettle took what was left of his people and camped as far away from troops as he could. Four years after Sand Creek, Colonel George Armstrong Custer, in his first Indian battle, attacked the camp with his seventh cavalry, and massacred forty more of the Cheyenne. In 1870 troops descended on a Blackfeet camp in Montana, "leaving 173 men, women and children dead in the snow."[9] The next year in Arizona, eighty-five Apache, mostly women and children, were

Armed Conflict

Colonel George Armstrong Custer led his troops in an attack against the Cheyenne that left more than forty dead.

The RELOCATION of NATIVE PEOPLES of NORTH AMERICA

Colonel Custer employed Indians as scouts and guides. Shown here are Custer with Bloody Knife (kneeling left), Custer's favorite scout.

killed by settlers in what came to be known as the Camp Grant Massacre.

There was to be one more massive Indian war and one more massacre, among the many small skirmishes and atrocities that marked the late nineteenth century in the West. The Battle of the Little Big Horn, on June 25, 1876, which resulted from yet another reduction in hunting grounds for the Sioux, was a major defeat for the US Army. Sitting Bull and Crazy Horse led a force of nearly two thousand warriors, the largest assembly of Indian forces ever gathered on the Plains. It took the Indians just one hour to wipe out Custer's company of 210 soldiers, and not much longer to almost wipe out soldiers from a following company.

Armed Conflict

The Riel Rebellions

Under their leader Louis Riel the Métis took up arms twice to resist the Canadian government. In the Red River Rebellion (1869-1870) the Métis, who feared to lose their farms along the Red and Assiniboine rivers as settlers were pushing west, seized Fort Gary, a trading post of the Hudson Bay Company. The result of the conflict was the Manitoba Act of 1870, through which the province of the same name was created. The act guaranteed that the land the Métis occupied would not be taken from them.

In 1884 a group of Métis living in Batoche (located in what was then the Northwest Territories, today in Saskatchewan) asked Riel to help them treat with the Canadian government to secure their land rights. As the government proved less willing to negotiate than in 1870, the Métis seized the church at Bastoche and formed a provisional government with Riel as president, starting the North-West Rebellion of 1885. After two months of fighting the Canadian troops overwhelmed the Métis, and Riel was executed for treason.[10]

62 The RELOCATION of NATIVE PEOPLES of NORTH AMERICA

This depiction of the Battle of the Little Bighorn was painted by Amos Bad Heart Bull, an Oglala Sioux from the Pine Ridge reservation.

Though this was a major victory for the Sioux, the shock of the complete loss of a company and its leader set the stage for a massive upsurge in military pursuit of all the Indians in the area. As the Indians were rounded up and sent to reservations, punishment in the form of reduced food and clothing rations was common. Soldiers who were frightened by his presence murdered Chief Crazy Horse after his surrender.[11]

Reduced to a Minority

When the treaty policy ended in 1871, 370 treaties, beginning in 1778, had been agreed upon between the US government and American Indians. The majority of those treaties were violated, not by the Indians, but by the whites. The idea that American Indians were considered sovereign peoples, with power to negotiate treaties, had ended, with horrendous consequences for America's original inhabitants.

Indians on reservations were included for the first time in the 1890 census. By that year, the population of the United States was sixty-three million. The Indian population, estimated at around five million in 1600, was only 237,000. George L. Russell, writer, demographer, and a Saginaw Chippewa wrote: "In fewer than one hundred years, Indian tribal lands had been reduced [from] all land west of the Appalachian Mountains to desolate reservations totaling less than four percent of the continental United States."[12]

Utmost Good Faith?

The utmost good faith shall always be observed towards the Indians; their lands and property shall never be taken without their consent; and in their property, rights, and liberty, they shall never be invaded or disturbed, unless in just and lawful wars authorized by Congress; but laws founded in justice and humility shall from time to time be made for preventing wrongs being done to them, and for preserving peace and friendship with them.[13]

Chapter 7

Indian Suffering

The Natives who survived the diseases and armed conflicts had to endure great changes in their lives. Indian spiritual beliefs had always been a part of every day, of everything from hunting to communal ritual. In order to bring some sense back to their world, various tribes looked for spiritual guidance and help, often combining Christian beliefs with their old ways of spiritual connection.

Religion as Refuge

Wovoka, a Paiute prophet, preached a message of hope that included prayer, rejection of alcohol, and ceremonial purification as the way to bring back the old way of life. Do not mourn, he said, the future can have hope. There will be a future that brings back the buffalo and without white men in it to harm you.[1]

The major component of the ceremonial purification was the Ghost Dance. Indians from across the Plains, particularly the Sioux, Cheyenne, and

Indian Suffering

Arapaho, came together to sing and sway, wearing special "ghost" shirts that were supposed to make them safe against bullets. The dance allowed them to enter trances in which they experienced a happier future.

White settlers knew of this Ghost Dance and became alarmed by the idea of American Indians dancing wildly and talking of the disappearance of white men. Searching for the leaders of this spiritual movement, agents of the Bureau of Indian Affairs killed Sitting Bull and seven ghost dancers. Word, and alarm, spread among the Indians and the whites. The revitalization of spiritual movements, such as the Ghost Dance, led to the tragedy at Wounded Knee.

Spiritual Movement

George Sword, an Oglala Sioux, describes the Ghost Dance as follows:

> The persons in the ghost dancing all joined hands. A man stands and then a woman, so in that way forming a very large circle. They dance around in the circle in a continuous time until some of them become so tired and overtired that they became crazy and finally drop as though dead.[2]

The RELOCATION of NATIVE PEOPLES of NORTH AMERICA

American Indians performed the Ghost Dance as a way of purification.

The Wounded Knee Massacre

A Sioux leader named Big Foot led his followers, which included around four hundred men, women, and children, to the Pine Ridge reservation. Their purpose was to arrange a meeting with other Sioux leaders.

On December 28, 1890, the Seventh Cavalry, with five hundred soldiers, met Big Foot's group, who were ordered to camp at Wounded Knee Creek. The next morning all the Sioux men were told to line up and give up their weapons. "As a deaf Sioux called Black Coyote was struggling to hold on to his rifle a shot was heard (it is still not clear which side it came from) and the nervous cavalry opened fire," says James Wilson.[3]

One of Big Foot's warriors who survived the massacre was Wasumaza (who later changed his name

Indian Suffering

to Dewey Beard). He gave an eyewitness account of the beginning of the slaughter. His account appears in *Bury My Heart at Wounded Knee*, by Dee Brown:

> If they had left him [Black Coyote] alone he was going to put his gun down where he should . . . He hadn't his gun pointed at anyone. . . . They came on and grabbed the gun that he was going to put down. Right after they spun him around there was the report of a gun, quite loud.[4]

Because of the cavalry's powerful rapid-fire weapons called Hotchkiss guns, the Sioux men were killed immediately. The soldiers continued to fire as some Indians fought back with whatever they had on hand while others tried to run away. About two hundred people were killed within an hour and others were pursued by the soldiers as they fled. Around one hundred made it to the nearby hills where they later froze to death.

Though the massacre at Wounded Knee might have been the *coup de grace* (or final blow) to large-scale Indian rebellion and peaceful protest in the nineteenth century, other forces may have been more devastating. According to one historian, "The devastation wrought by disease and the expropriation of their land through the bloodless process of treaty making and anti-Indian legislation" were the major causes of loss of freedom for all the tribes.[5]

Land Ownership

The Dawes Act, or the General Allotment Act passed in 1887, created more pressure for American Indian

68 The RELOCATION of NATIVE PEOPLES of NORTH AMERICA

After the tragedy at Wounded Knee, bodies of Sioux Indians were unceremoniously piled into a mass grave.

Indian Suffering

lands and contributed to the climate in which incidents like Wounded Knee could occur. Ever since white settlers came to North America and began wanting to own specific parcels of land, they had looked down on the Indian notion of using land in common. The concept of private ownership of land was completely foreign to Indians, who believed that land was not something to be owned. Though certain areas were considered tribal hunting territories, this was far different from individual "ownership" of a piece of the earth. Europeans simply did not understand, and certainly did not respect, the idea of a group of people who spoke of land as "ours."

Dividing land into plots owned by a single family was a popular practice at this time. Many people believed that the only way to "save" the Indians was to make them act like everybody else, with the same customs and daily lives as white people, and they thought single-plot ownership was the key. The Bureau of Indian Affairs thought it could reduce the bill for food and services required by former treaties on the reservations. They also knew they could profit by selling whatever reservation land was left after the single-plot subdivision. Even Indians who had managed to have some power in the white world, including Indian commissioner Ely Parker, believed that private land ownership would help Indians gain a higher standard of living than seemed possible at that time.

But there were many pitfalls in this argument. First, there was no guarantee as to the quality of land taken

The RELOCATION of NATIVE PEOPLES of NORTH AMERICA

Ely Parker, Iroquois Indian chief and Commissioner for Indian Affairs, approved of dividing reservation land into plots and distributing allotments to the American Indians.

Indian Suffering

from the common reservation. Many of these reservations were located on dry soil that could not support agriculture. And if it was good land, what was to stop the constant land hunger that sent settlers surging through Indian lands? What was to stop these private plots from falling into the hands of land speculators who offered to buy them from hungry, discouraged Indians?

The Indian population had shrunk alarmingly over the years. But if families were settled on small private plots, and if the death rate from murder, disease, and hunger was reduced, there might be more Indians, not fewer. No one considered that, if allotment brought about the improved conditions for Indians that it was supposed to, the Indian population might increase. In the Great Lakes region an allotment was eighty acres and sometimes only forty acres. In the West the land allotment was 160 acres and occasionally 320 acres. What would happen to those plots of land when they had to be divided among the heirs—children and grandchildren—of the families who owned them? They would, of course, become smaller and, eventually, too small to support the families who farmed them.

Some Indians accepted allotment as inevitable, whether they believed it would be beneficial to them or not. "Many tribes, however, put up stiff resistance." says historian James Wilson.[6] Southwestern nations asked for help from the better organized groups like the Cherokee, Chickasaw, Choctaw, Creek, Seminole, and the Osage, whose lands—still not being called a

72 The RELOCATION of NATIVE PEOPLES of NORTH AMERICA

Senator Henry Dawes was the author of the Dawes Act, which broke up reservations into allotments for Indian families. Much of the land, however, ended up in the hands of white settlers.

Indian Suffering

reservation—were not part of the allotment plan. A committee of twenty-two Indian nations met to try to unite as one Indian government to fight allotment.

The committee set about drafting a constitution for an Indian Union. However, before it could meet again, the US government had forced the sale of two million acres of land belonging to the Cherokee, Chickasaw, Choctaw, Creek, and Seminole nations. The next year, their former land was reorganized as Oklahoma Territory, open to white settlement. The Cherokee and other tribes were forced onto a small part of their former lands, their successful farms and schools closed.

In other areas, resistance was less obvious, but the discontent was apparent to white settlers. In the Northwest, the Commissioner of Indian Affairs ordered that no Indians leave the reservation without permission. If too much grumbling occurred, the Bureau of Indian affairs withheld government food, clothing, and other supplies, on which the tribes had become dependent. And if there was more trouble, the army could be called in to subdue protest. The growing strength of the Ghost Dance movement, which preceded the massacre at Wounded Knee, occurred during resistance to the Dawes Act.

Surplus land, that is land that once was part of a reservation, was put up for sale to white settlers. "This action was in direct violation of the treaty agreements," says Indian author George Russell. "Prior to the Allotment Act tribal land holdings totaled 138 million acres. By the end of the allotment period in

The RELOCATION of NATIVE PEOPLES of NORTH AMERICA

White settlers rush to claim land in what would become Oklahoma Territory in September 1893.

1934, nearly 90 million acres held passed out of Indian tribal ownership."[7] Massive land transfers occurred through lotteries, sealed bids, and "runs," something that became famous in Western movies. Anyone wanting to stake a claim to former Indian land could start at a fixed point, in a wagon or on a horse or mule, and "run" to claim land. Two million acres of treaty-held Indian lands were confiscated using this method.

In 1890 former Cherokee and other American Indian lands in present-day Oklahoma became home to sixty thousand whites. Ten years later, the white population was four hundred thousand. By 1890, the government acquired 13 million acres; by 1891, 23 million acres; by 1892, 30 million acres—all former reservation land.[8]

Indian Suffering

The Dawes Act allowed for a phenomenon known as checkerboarding, or mixed land ownership. Land on many reservations came to look like a checkerboard, with land owned by Indian individuals, non-Indian individuals or groups, the state, the county, and the federal government. According to the treaties that created the reservations, all land within the boundaries of the reservation was supposed to be owned by the American Indians settled there.

Exploitation of Trust

Often American Indians avoided confrontation by retreating into areas that seemed unwanted by white settlers. There they could continue to live at least somewhat according to their own customs. The White River Utes left their reservation and headed for South Dakota. The Kickapoo in western Indian Territory, when faced with dividing their reservation into allotments, gave all their money to a lawyer who promised to buy them land in Mexico. He, along with several other government figures, took the money and never purchased land. This left the Kickapoo in great poverty and forced them to accept the allotment system.

The RELOCATION of NATIVE PEOPLES of NORTH AMERICA

It was not only the loss of land that was caused by allotment. The idea of lands parceled out to individuals who were then expected to farm them in the white man's way, changed age-old cultural practices. Reservations were each assigned to a Christian denomination and Indian religious rituals were suppressed, often violently.

As Charlotte Black Elk, Lakota Sioux says:

> All of a sudden we were told: Not only will you not be able to practice your religion, but you shall also bring all of your sacred objects—sacred pipes, spirit bundles, everything that we had that was sacred— into the agency and there we shall have a grand bonfire. Every little thing that told us we were Lakota and that was tied into our culture, our social fabric, was outlawed. [These practices were designed to say] everything about you is bad. So everything about our culture was systematically to be destroyed.[9]

Legal Development in Canada

After Canada had become an independent nation, the government regulated its relation with the Aboriginals in several pieces of legislation. Modeled after the Robinson Treaties of 1850, Canada undertook a series of eleven land surrender treaties, referred to as the Numbered Treaties, which opened new land for settlers in what are now Alberta, British Columbia, Manitoba, Ontario, Saskatchewan, and the Northwest Territories. The first seven of the Numbered Treaties were concluded between 1871 and 1877, while the last of them was agreed upon in 1921.

Indian Suffering

The Dakota Indians perform a traditional dance. Many American Indian customs and rituals were outlawed in an attempt to make the native people more like white people.

In exchange for the land surrendered, other areas were set aside as reserves to be under the control of the First Nations, Canadian Aboriginal people who were neither Inuit nor Métis. The First Nations would also receive annual compensation, usually in the form of money, hunting or farming equipment, or food. These arrangements helped take care of their people in a time where hunting was no longer a viable means of subsistence as the buffalo neared extinction and the fur traders were driven further northwards. Therefore, the leaders signing the treaties approved of this process. Schools were established and the Indians

The RELOCATION of NATIVE PEOPLES of NORTH AMERICA

The Potlatch

Potlatches were ceremonies held to mark weddings, births, and other social events. These celebrations could last for days, and in addition to a great feast, generous gifts would be exchanged. The potlatch ceremony was important to the Indians of the Northwest Pacific coast because it affirmed the rank and social status of the donors, but government agents and missionaries saw it as excessive and wasteful. Consequently, the practice was banned in Canada through an amendment to the Indian Act in 1884, and in the late nineteenth century it was prohibited in the United States as well, disrupting the cultural practices and traditions of the natives. The ban was lifted in the United States in 1934 and in Canada in 1951, and today these celebrations are held once again.[10]

Indian Suffering

Kwakiutl Indians participate in a potlatch ceremony at Fort Rupert, Canada.

were encouraged to take up a sedentary way of life and become farmers.

The government desire to "civilize" the Indians also led to the Indian Act of 1876, a piece of legislation that consolidated earlier laws and gave more authority to the Department of Indian Affairs. The management of Indian lands and moneys was laid in the hands of the Department, and rather than leaving it up to the Aboriginal groups themselves, the Indian Act defined who was or was not an Indian. For example, Métis and Aboriginal women who married non-Indians were now denied Indian status. The government now

The RELOCATION of NATIVE PEOPLES of NORTH AMERICA

grew more involved with groups that had once been regarded as autonomous nations, acting as guardians to protect the Indians from themselves and others until they were assimilated into Canadian society.

One tool to achieve the desired integration was the system that allowed Aboriginals to give up their Indian status and gain full citizenship if they met certain criteria. Few Indians chose this option, though. As a consequence, the Indian Act was changed in 1880, so that any First Nations member who received a university degree became a citizen and lost their Indian status, whether they wanted to or not. Over the course of the following fifty years many changes were made to the Indian Act to further the "civilization" and give the government more control.[10]

Chapter 8

Forced Assimilation

In an attempt to assimilate Indians into the culture the government deemed acceptable, American Indian schools were introduced on reservations as early as 1879. Individual ownership of land was one thing, but what the American government thought really needed to happen was the education of the Indian in the exact same way as white children. However, this education would not stop at English grammar and mathematics. Before this could happen, the children would be forced to not speak their native tongue and to give up the long hair and loose (and comfortable) dress of their people. The network of residential boarding schools established in Canada after 1880 followed the same goal of assimilating Aboriginal children into a culture shaped by Christian and European values foreign to them.

The RELOCATION of NATIVE PEOPLES of NORTH AMERICA

Schools as a Tool for "Civilizing"

The first Indian school, which became a model for others, was the Carlisle Indian School in Pennsylvania. It was founded by Captain Richard Pratt, who believed that Indian children needed to achieve an entirely new identity. In one of his many pronouncements, he stated his major aim in this slogan, "Kill the Indian and save the man!"[1] Though Pratt was not among the many whites who believed that American Indians were an inferior race who deserved to be killed, he believed that everything about their culture must be destroyed in order to "civilize" the children he and others would teach.

When children arrived at the school they had their hair cut very short or often had their heads shaved. They put on uncomfortable uniforms and tight-waisted dresses and were marched in military drill. They were given English names. They were forbidden to speak their own language, and severely punished, sometimes beaten and disfigured, if they forgot to speak English.

The food was perhaps one of the most difficult adjustments. In some schools, instead of simple meat and soup and some vegetables, they were fed a diet of white bread, coffee, and sugar. This poor diet, coupled with tuberculosis, influenza, and other ailments, caused the death of many Indian children. At the end of the first three years at the Carlisle Indian School, "nearly one half of the children from the Plains were dead and through with all earthly schools. In the

Forced Assimilation

This group of Apache students attended the Carlisle Indian School. They were not allowed to wear traditional Indian dress at school.

graveyard at Carlisle most of the graves were those of little ones," remembers Luther Standing Bear, one of the first Carlisle pupils.[2]

Publicity about the school painted a very different picture than the true one of suffering. Educating Indian children became a popular occupation for teachers from many different Christian faiths. Since breaking down the culture was thought to be an important part of assimilation, most of these schools were boarding schools where the parents were not allowed to visit.

84 The RELOCATION of NATIVE PEOPLES of NORTH AMERICA

These photos show Tom Torlino before and after he started attending Carlisle Indian School.

Forced Assimilation

A few families were successful at hiding their children so that they never entered the degrading system. Many children forced to enter the schools ran away and were severely punished when they were caught and returned. Thousands of children died due to poor diet and disease, and some children seemed to just waste away from loneliness. Other children ended up becoming good students, and entering the white man's world, where they faced discrimination in employment. Others were able to bring their learning back to their people and still respect the old ways. Most of those who survived, however, were confused as to which culture to embrace.

In 2007 the Canadian Government implemented the Indian Residential School Settlement Agreement, a $1.9 billion package to compensate former students of the abusive residential school system. In 2008 Prime Minister Stephen Harper apologized on behalf of Canada for the fact that more than 150,000 Aboriginal children had been taken from their families and forced to attend these schools, the last of which closed as late as 1996.[3]

Changing Relations

To fully understand what the reservations were like, it is necessary to review the relatively short history of American Indian and European relations in North America.

The progression to total dependence on the government had three phases. Early on, Indian groups were recognized as sovereign nations. For instance,

The RELOCATION of NATIVE PEOPLES of NORTH AMERICA

The Assembly of First Nations chief responds to Canada's official apology, given at the House of Commons in 2008, for a century of mistreatment and abuse.

the United States and the Iroquois Confederacy existed side by side as equal powers. As more and more land was taken away from American Indians, they began to be considered domestic dependent nations, no longer an equal power. If the United States and, respectively, the British colonies that would become Canada, had other nations living within it, then it became the responsibility of the government to protect the members of those nations. The treaties made with these nations were always broken. (This became important in the twentieth century because treaties are legal documents, and American Indians began to seek legal enforcement of old treaties.)

Forced Assimilation

Finally, the whole idea of separate nations disappeared as the land owned and lived on by Indians became smaller. The Plains Indians could no longer feed themselves because the buffalo were gone (by 1900 there were thirty-nine buffalo in Yellowstone National Park[4]) and the land used for all game hunting was filled with settlers.

An example of how the land for reservations was whittled away is what happened to the Western Sioux. Their original reservation was designated as all of South Dakota west of the Mississippi River. They also had treaty-negotiated hunting rights in Montana and Wyoming. When gold was discovered in the Black Hills of South Dakota, the government offered to buy the area from the Sioux. When they refused, they were forced onto the reservation. The Battle of the Little Big Horn followed.

A Lakota Sioux camp near the Pine Ridge reservation in South Dakota.

The RELOCATION of NATIVE PEOPLES of NORTH AMERICA

This political cartoon shows the corrupt agent profiting while the Sioux Indian starves.

Pursued relentlessly after their victory at Little Big Horn, the Sioux ended up by losing a full third of their reservation and all their hunting rights in Montana and Wyoming. The next reduction came when settlers complained to the government about the Sioux reservation being in the way of their emigration to eastern Dakota. The Sioux were then forced to create a sixty-mile-wide corridor right through the middle and the farthest western portion of their reservation. The remainder was divided up into the five small reservations they occupy today. And that was not all—the Dawes Act was enacted and the remaining reservation was divided into 160-acre parcels and what was left over was sold to whites.[5]

Forced Assimilation

On the Sioux and almost all other reservations, Indians had no way to work or hunt for their own food. Many reservations had rules that would not allow American Indians to leave the boundaries. The reservation Indians became totally dependent on government rations. They lost a sense of purpose, hope, and self-esteem and were reduced often to begging and petty stealing just to fill their stomachs. They suffered tuberculosis and other diseases, malnutrition, and alcoholism. The government rations were often cut in half or replaced with spoiled food and shoddy goods because of widespread corruption among officials and agents employed by the Bureau of Indian Affairs. Though there were a few good and honest agents, they were often removed because the middlemen who supplied the reservations wanted to continue to put the money in their own pockets.

Economic Difficulties

Reservations became places of chronic poverty, with no work available. "In the decade after the Civil War, behind-the-scenes corruption in the Indian Bureau went from bad to worse," says Peter Nabokov.[6] Members of Congress, dishonest suppliers of the food and other goods, and Indian agents often came up with schemes to divert the money owed to the reservations.

In 1867 a group of citizens from the Eastern states formed the Indian Peace Commission, to find out if the shocking rumors of poverty and poor health on the reservations were true. In 1871 President Grant

The RELOCATION of NATIVE PEOPLES of NORTH AMERICA

A missionary stands with four American Indians in 1896.

launched a similar investigation through the Board of Indian Commissioners, which would oversee the Bureau of Indian Affairs. These civilian groups discovered that many of the Indians were near starvation because corrupt agents had stolen the money allocated for buying supplies for the reservation.

Many of the corrupt agents were replaced with leaders of various Christian religious denominations. Some of the worst conditions were changed for the better. Often, however, the religious groups, which divided the tribes between them, were more interested in converting the Indians to Christianity than in alleviating their immediate suffering.

Forced Assimilation

At least one Quaker missionary was remembered as a true leader by an Arapaho artist named Carl Sweezy, who lived on a reservation in Oklahoma: "There was more than one white man's road that we might take, and President Grant wanted us to take the right one. He sent Brinton Darlington to be our first Agent." Darlington brought other Quakers with him who helped plant orchards and gardens, and built good housing, schools, and trading posts. "He was patient and kind; he managed like a chief," says Sweezy.[7]

A young anthropologist named Clark Wissler, who later became Curator of Ethnology at the American Museum of Natural History, traveled around the country west of the Mississippi for several years at the turn of the century. His portraits of Indians and early reservation life, while retaining the superior attitude toward a different race that was typical of white men of his generation, are compassionate and detailed. In one piece of writing he presents a report made by an agent at the Blackfeet reservation in Montana in 1884:

> When I entered upon the duties of agent, I found the Indians in a deplorable condition. Their supplies had been limited and many of them were gradually dying of starvation. I visited a large number of their tents and cabins the second day after they had received their weekly rations.... All bore marks of suffering from lack of food but the little children seemed to have suffered most; they were so emaciated that it did not seem possible for them to live long; and many of them have since passed away.[8]

The RELOCATION of NATIVE PEOPLES of NORTH AMERICA

This agent was clearly appalled by the situation and by the fact that the reservation simply did not receive enough food for the twenty-three hundred Indians who lived there. He was forced to open and use food that had been condemned, and he reported that Indians were reduced to stripping bark from trees along the creeks and eating the inner portion because they were so hungry. These were people who had hunted the buffalo, by then almost extinct. "This great economic and spiritual depression involved far more tribes than had been caught up in the toils of any other reservation calamity," says Wissler.[9]

The entire economy of the tribes had collapsed. "For confronting the Indian was a forbidding and uninspiring outlook. No longer could he look forward to the long hunting expeditions so dear to him, but

Buffalo Bill's Wild West show used American Indians for entertainment. It did not convey the hardships they faced.

Forced Assimilation

what was worse all the worthy aspirations and ambitions sanctioned by his culture were thwarted."[10]

Conditions on the reservations gradually improved in the last years of the nineteenth century. The threat of Indian uprisings had ended. The Indian became, thanks to pulp magazine stories and Buffalo Bill's Wild West show, which staged Indian fights, part of the "romantic West" mythology. What was happening to the real Indian was never part of this mythology. The former "owners" of America were living out their lives on various reservations, and continuing, as best they could, their own customs.

Life on a Reservation

American Indians on the early reservations still lived in tipis, longhouses, hogans, and other Indian homes as often as they could. They also liked to get permission to visit far away reservations. In the Plains, they would load their tipis and equipment on travois (a kind of sled made of poles, which was pulled by horses or dogs), and camp along the way. This enabled them to live in the old way, with each other and without the agent and the store, at least for a short time.

On each reservation was the agency store. Here Indians gathered to spend whatever money they had been allotted, though some goods were still traded. Since most Indians in the early reservation days could not read or write, they were at the mercy of the trader when they handed over a check for goods. Having been cheated so many times by dishonest traders, the Indian shopper was distrustful of everyone. Since

The RELOCATION of NATIVE PEOPLES of NORTH AMERICA

Four Lakota Sioux women stand with a Lakota man on horseback on the Pine Ridge Reservation in South Dakota.

leaving the reservation required a permit, the Indian had little opportunity to spend money in a town. The trader and the high price of goods kept him in debt. The life of the reservation centered around the store, where much-needed blankets, clothing, and food could help against the constant hunger and cold.

The dispensing of medicine was another of the many difficulties found on the reservation. Indians had completely different ideas about illness and death than those of white people. Traveling doctors, often much respected by their Indian patients, found that the concept of medical prescriptions was difficult to get across. If, after the first dose of medicine, the

Forced Assimilation

patient was not feeling much better, he would refuse to take any more. When a medicine to be rubbed on the skin was left with the patient, if it felt good, the rest often was used all at once. Similarly, if cough medicine was given and it did not taste too bad, the whole bottle would be drunk at once. The reasoning was that if it worked, it should all be used.

Wissler made many Indian friends in his travels, and his observations broadened his perspective on their value systems: "It is not difficult to realize . . . that though a white man and an Indian may walk side by side, they do not see alike . . . each may justly regard the other as a fool."[11]

Chapter 9

Buyout of Indian Land

A few rebellions, led by young American Indian men, still happened on the outskirts of reservations in the West between 1890 and 1915. For the most part, these young Indians were bored and confused, and had no elders to guide them in the kind of leadership their people needed. Occasionally, during this time, sightings were reported by hikers of lone Indians disappearing into dense underbrush, often in California where whites had practiced "Indian hunts." There were no reservations in California, and the few Indians left pretended to be Latino so they could make a living as seasonal workers.

From Indian Territory to Oklahoma Territory

The bulk of Indian people during this era were struggling with the effects of the Dawes Act and living on the reservations. In 1897 President William McKinley announced that Indian Territory would become part of the United States. Through outright stealing and

Buyout of Indian Land

land grabs, what remained of Indian lands was lost. The certainty that even a small parcel of land would be safe from white land grabbing decreased with each new administration.

In 1901 an act was passed that allowed roads to be built through an allotment. If an Indian's land happened to be in the way of the road, the land would be condemned and returned to government use. This action is called eminent domain and is still occasionally taken against Americans today. "The thrust of government policy remained aimed at negating any sense of cultural wholeness," says Nabokov.[1] Another act in 1907 allowed the government to distribute money that was supposed to be for American Indian

An Indian encampment in Oklahoma Territory. At the start of the twentieth century, the American Indians continued to lose land as white settlers grabbed all that they could.

nations to individuals, thus once again reducing the idea of shared land and assets.

In Indian Territory, where Cherokee and other "removed" Indians had made a new and prosperous home, much land had already been taken away by the government. Indian Territory then became Oklahoma Territory. (Oklahoma did not become a state until 1907.) When the Dawes Act was passed in 1887, nineteen Indian Territory tribes had voted against it. They now fought for an all-Indian state to be named after Sequoyah, the Cherokee who had invented his people's alphabet. They lost this fight, and yet as late as 1912, two thousand Cherokee, though living in terrible poverty, still refused to claim their allotments. Even those who did move onto allotments had no security. The problem of inheritance, as heirs tried to divide the small parcels of land between them, meant there was simply not enough land left on which to make a living.

The Impact of World War I

When oil was discovered on the lands of the Osage, Creek, Seminole, and Delaware tribes, land grabbers went to quite incredible lengths to obtain deeds to Indian lands. "False wills were drafted. Indian family members were bribed, beatings and even murder were not uncommon," says Nabokov.[2]

Of the thirty million acres deeded to Indian individuals during allotment, only three million were left by 1920. By 1956 members of the Cherokee, Chickasaw, Choctaw, Creek, and Seminole nations owned only 326,902 acres of trust land. This was 1.6 percent of

Buyout of Indian Land

the territory they had been promised they would live on "forever," which had been still intact as of 1898.[3]

It may seem odd that Indians, who had been systematically pursued, killed, cheated, and confined by the government would be willing to go to war for the United States and Canada in World War I. Some wanted access to the high status that could come with combat experience. Some wanted adventure and opportunity. Some felt patriotic toward their country. Or perhaps it was the chance to be an active part of almost anything, instead of sitting

Splitting the Land

Historian Peter Nabokov uses this example to illustrate the problem of allotments:

Lizette Denomie was a Chippewa allottee who died in 1897. Her eighty-acre plot was split up among nine heirs. Twenty years later six of them had died, subdividing the land further so that fourteen of these third-generation heirs had only patches of between four-and-a half acres to three-quarters of an acre apiece. Finally, in 1935, the original tract had been splintered among thirty-five heirs, seventeen of them expected to make a living on less than an acre each.[4]

The RELOCATION of NATIVE PEOPLES of NORTH AMERICA

around a reservation getting inadequate handouts. The reasons that drove twenty-five thousand young Indian men to join the United States army and navy and six thousand to serve in the Canadian Armed Forces varied.

Even more remarkable is that ten thousand Indian Red Cross volunteers, almost all women, sewed one hundred thousand pieces of clothing for overseas troops. They also made sure that five hundred Christmas boxes were sent abroad. Despite their poverty, Indians bought twenty-five million dollars in war bonds.[5]

Designated for the highest French honor for bravery was Joseph Oklahombi, a Choctaw Indian from Wright City, Oklahoma. Oklahombi was one of the Choctaw code talkers, one of the first groups to use American Indian language as military code. This extraordinary soldier used the same incredible courage, speed, and athletic ability that had threatened US troops during the Indian Wars, to run through seemingly impenetrable barbed wire and open trenches to overpower machine-gun nests as a US soldier during World War I. Oklahombi captured German prisoners, pinpointed strategic enemy strongholds, and rescued wounded soldiers.

While Indians were demonstrating their skills and their loyalty to the war effort, the economic impact of the war harmed the tribes at home. Indian lands were the first to lose funding if the government needed extra money for wartime needs.

Buyout of Indian Land

Choctaw code talkers used their own language to encode radio and telephone transimissions for the U.S. military during WWI.

However, change was coming. The deplorable conditions at the Indian boarding schools, which included widespread tuberculosis and an eye infection called trachoma, began to be noticed. The Society of American Indians and the Federal Indian Health program, founded in 1906 and 1908, respectively, worked hard to bring healthier conditions to these schools. Despite the cruel conditions, some of the graduates retained their pride in their Indian heritage and also learned the skills to make a positive impact in the world. Further improvements for American Indians were initiated after World War I by a dedicated white man, social reformer John Collier.

Ishi, Last of the Yahi Yana

The very last member of the Yahi Yana tribe was discovered by barking dogs near a corral in Oroville, California, on August 9, 1911. He was put in jail, but was rescued from local ranchers by scholars T.T. Waterman and A. L. Kroeber. Ishi, as the man came to be called, had escaped the massacres of the 1860s and 1870s. Since then he had been hiding in the mountain terrain. Treated kindly, Ishi helped the ethnographers with knowledge of his soon-to-be extinct tribe.

When Ishi died in 1916, Waterman wrote a tribute to Ishi, saying:

> He had an innate regard for the other fellow's existence, and an inborn considerateness . . . to know him was a rare personal privilege, not merely an ethnological privilege. I feel myself that in many ways he was perhaps the most remarkable personality of his century.[6]

Buyout of Indian Land

The last surviving member of the Yahi Yana tribe of northern California, called Ishi, photographed in 1914.

Chapter 10

Steps Toward Multiculturalism

John Collier, a Commissioner for the Bureau of Indian Affairs (BIA), did not agree with one goal of the Dawes Act. Instead of trying to force all people to live the same way and have the same customs, he believed in multiculturalism. He thought that all the different peoples of the United States should keep their own traditional customs, languages, music, and religion. He believed that human beings needed the experience, the ritual, and spiritual joining of a true community in order to lead fulfilled lives.

Public Protest

Collier's early reform efforts were aimed at immigrants in large cities. When he was introduced through a friend to the Pueblo Indians, whose reservation is in New Mexico, he was fascinated. The very communal experience that legislation such as the Dawes Act had tried to kill in the native population was, for Collier, what human beings needed to survive. He did not

Steps Toward Multiculturalism

John Collier was a social reformer who believed that American Indians should retain their unique culture and lifestyle.

believe that this communal American Indian spirit was doomed to extinction and he intended to help revive it.

The Pueblo Indians were well-organized farmers who lived quietly, so they were not regulated severely by the US government. Through a complex interweaving of old treaties and new legislation, the Pueblo Indians found themselves about to lose title to some lands and much of their water rights and soon would face massive federal regulation. The Bursum Bill before Congress in 1922, which would hand over Pueblo land to non-Indians, would have destroyed the Pueblo culture.

The RELOCATION of NATIVE PEOPLES of NORTH AMERICA

By this time, John Collier was working with the Pueblo, along with white artists and writers who had settled in New Mexico and appreciated the Pueblo way of life. Collier organized a protest, sending Pueblo singers and dancers on tour across the country, including large cities such as Chicago and New York, on their way to Washington, D.C., Indians, having had their lands taken, were being looked at very differently in the twentieth century than in the nineteenth. A large public protest in the form of letters and telegrams flooded the White House in support of the Pueblo's position. In March 1923, the Bursum Bill's supporters stopped trying to get it passed.

Critical View of the Administration

The BIA, however, continued to attack the religious and cultural practices of all tribes, particularly the Pueblo and the Hopi. In answer to this attack, Collier formed the American Indian Defense Association (AIDA), which pledged to preserve Indian religion and the dances and other rituals associated with it. He faced great opposition from Christian religious groups who still wanted to "civilize" the Indians. Collier's great determination finally won out and along the way he gathered and publicized information about the BIA's mishandling of rations, health, and education on the reservations.

The director of the Institute for Government Research, Lewis Meriam, conducted an investigation that he published in *The Problem of Indian Administration*. The Meriam report came out in 1928, right

Steps Toward Multiculturalism

Navajo women on a New Mexico reservation work the wool, spin yarn, and weave the yarn into rugs to sell to tourists.

before the stock market crash and the beginning of the Great Depression. Meriam's report condemned the Dawes Act and allotment system not only as a total failure, but the cause of the terrible financial burden on the nation from the inefficient and corrupt BIA.

The Indian Reorganization Act

Reacting to the Great Depression, when many people lost their jobs and suffered from extreme poverty, President Franklin Delano Roosevelt initiated reforms that became known as the New Deal. Elected in 1932, Roosevelt appointed John Collier as the commissioner of the Bureau of Indian Affairs, the same agency Collier had been battling for ten years. Collier used the Meriam Report to initiate the 1934 Indian Reorganization Act (IRA), which ended allotment. This would create its own difficulties. The act could not easily overturn the many years of adjusting to the allotment system and the breakdown of group unity that it brought about on some reservations.

Collier believed that going back to the idea that everyone in an American Indian group shared use of the land equally was the basis of the kind of community that could save the tribes. However, "The Dawes Act had left many reservations hopelessly checkerboarded and fragmented. Often, the best land had been removed from trust status and sold," says historian James Wilson.[1]

Collier managed to get his bill through Congress, but not without great difficulty. Many of the IRA's best

Steps Toward Multiculturalism

John Collier stands with Indian chiefs in 1934.

provisions were difficult to implement, but would lead to future reforms and tribal self-governance.

Collier quickly managed to bring about an Indian New Deal within the larger New Deal reforms. The need to cut down on government spending helped Collier and other reformers bring more self-sufficiency to reservation government. However, Collier and his reforms were often looked on as too controlling. "Struggles over how tribes should be governed and by whom have been present since the inception of the Indian Reorganization Act," says historian George Russell.[2]

Reorganization and Revision

There were several reforms in the Indian Reorganization Act that were designed to correct some of the damage done to American Indian societies.
1. All further allotment was prohibited.
2. Money was set aside to buy more land for the American Indians.
3. Money was allocated for the tribes to set up business corporations, and they were encouraged to form their own governments.

After Canada had signed the United Nations Universal Declaration of Human Rights in 1948, the government examined its policy in regard to the Aboriginals, who were clearly disadvantaged. As a result, Canada's Indian Act was revised in 1951, and some of the most oppressive sections were taken out. Cultural practices like the potlatch were no longer banned, Indians were allowed to wear their traditional dress outside their reserves without needing permission, and they were no longer forbidden to enter pool halls or gamble. The overall policy did not change, though, leaving a lot of control over the Aboriginal peoples in the hands of the government.

It took another nine years before Aboriginals were extended the right to vote in federal elections without having to give up their Indian status, and in 1961 the Indian Act was amended so that Indian status could not automatically be lost when certain criteria were met.

In 1969 the government made a proposal, commonly referred to as the White Paper, to abolish the Indian Act and end the separation between the Aboriginal peoples and the rest of Canadian society. This was perceived as another attempt at assimilation. While the Indian Act was seen as paternalistic, it also protected the special rights and benefits of the First Nations. The criticism of Aboriginal and non-Aboriginal people alike led the government to back away from its position and change its approach. Bill C-31 passed in 1985 removed discriminatory elements from the Indian Act, restored Indian status who had lost it involuntarily, and granted bands control over their own membership.[3]

Steps Toward Multiculturalism

A First Nations camp in Alberta, Canada, around 1920. Throughout the 1900s, the Aboriginal people slowly regained the rights they had lost through previous legislation.

Though Collier is much admired, he remains a controversial figure for many Indian and non-Indian peoples. (For instance, he ordered the destruction of thousands of Navajo sheep. Consequently, the Navajo never adopted the IRA and did not reorganize their government until much later.) Sometimes, in his romantic views of the communal life, he misunderstood "the enormous diversity of [American Indian] culture . . . [and that] as a result of Euro-American contact, most tribes had lost far more of their own traditions than the Pueblos and that some had changed so much" that they really had almost disappeared, according to historian James Wilson.[4]

The RELOCATION of NATIVE PEOPLES of NORTH AMERICA

Some Success in the Modern World

During the years leading up to the reforms John Collier supported, some Indians left the reservation to make their living in the white world. Indians all around the country were distinguishing themselves, despite discrimination.

In the 1920s, Mohawk Indians of the Caughnawaga tribe, living on a reservation in southern Canada, developed a high-risk, well-paid profession. Indians became the steelworkers who did the precision work on bridges and skyscrapers. They formed a neighborhood in Brooklyn of about two hundred to three hundred Mohawk, traveling back to the reservation for holidays and on most weekends. This group of Indians still participated in the cultural practices of their tribe but had managed to create a specialty that would support them monetarily in the modern world. Mohawk Indians still work together in the steel industry today.[5]

The all-around physical fitness and health of American Indians was far superior to their European conquerors—until diseases and bad housing and poverty took their toll. Athletes such as Jim Thorpe, the famous track star, and winning football teams from the Carlisle and Red Cloud Indian schools tapped into this natural athletic ability.

White reformers and artists who had left large cities to find new values in nature, often in the Southwest, appreciated the very Indian qualities earlier settlers had tried to destroy. However, this was largely

Steps Toward Multiculturalism

Jim Thorpe was a versatile athlete who excelled in many sports.

The RELOCATION of NATIVE PEOPLES of NORTH AMERICA

symbolic. Indians were looked on as people from the past, idealized romantically, and the individual Indian, struggling with poverty due to the corruption of the BIA in the reservation system, was mostly ignored. Indians still continued to lose land, lose their children to harsh boarding schools, and be expected to be farmers, even if they lived on desert-like land.

Historian Philip Deloria said:

> Here, then, is one of the paradoxes of Indian country in the twentieth century; if Indians change, their culture is considered contaminated and they lose their "Indianness." If they do not change, they remain Indians, but are refused a real existence in the modern world. . . . Defining oneself as an Indian in the twentieth century has meant walking a fine line between the domination and allure of American culture and the resistance and resilience of one's own tradition.[6]

Chapter 11

Political Movements

"I do not think the measure of a civilization is how tall its buildings of concrete are,

But rather how well its people have learned to relate to their environment and fellow man."

Sun Bear of the Chippewa Tribe[1]

The legislation of the Indian New Deal and the Indian Reorganization Act (IRA) saw some success in giving tribes more economic security on their reservations, but it also presented large challenges to Indian societies. American Indians were asked to form American-style governments that did not match well with their cultural practices. However, the IRA established Indian societies as dependent domestic nations with a right to govern their own people, which reaffirmed each nation's sovereignty. "It is, after all, a recognition in law of the fact that Indian societies were here first," remarks historian Philip Deloria.[2]

The RELOCATION of NATIVE PEOPLES of NORTH AMERICA

Employment Opportunities From the Depression to World War II

The Indian New Deal also created opportunities for paid labor on thirty-three reservations. The Indian Emergency Conservation Work (IECW) programs provided training and experience in money and resource management. During the Depression, when large numbers of people around the country were out of work and hungry, the IECW saved the lives of many Indian families. Eighty-five thousand Indians participated in the program and learned skills that would help them in off-reservation work, especially during World War II.[3]

John Collier had employed a great many Indians at the BIA before he resigned as its Commissioner in 1945. By then, both the Senate and the House of Representatives were again complaining that the BIA was spending too much money and had not completed the task of making reservations self-sufficient. Because the tribes had some skill in legal and political matters within their own reservations, they made an attempt to form an organization that would be a political forum for all tribes. In 1944 the National Congress of American Indians (NCAI) banded together to serve as a voice for the tribal nations.

Indians had acquired skills through programs put in place by the Indian New Deal and gained experience through their involvement in World War II. As in World War I, record numbers of American Indians joined the war effort. One third of all able-bodied

Political Movements

The Great Depression of the 1930s was devastating for the United States and Canada. Here, a long line of jobless and homeless men in New York wait outside for a free dinner.

//
Warriors in Modern Times

American Indian soldiers who served everywhere World War II was fought won many honors. Joseph Medicine Crow, a member of the Crow tribe, recalled his experience:

> When I went to Germany I never thought about war honors, or the four "coups" which an old-time Crow warrior had to earn in battle. Those days were gone. But afterwards, when I came back and went through this telling of the war deeds ceremony, why, I told my war deeds, and lo and behold I completed the four requirements to become a chief.[4]

The Choctaw telephone code talkers during World War I began the code talking tradition that continued in World War II. One of the most famous instances of Indian involvement in World War II was the Navajo Code Talkers. Though other tribes helped in encoding and deciphering for the army, such as the Oneida, Chippewa, Sauk, Fox, and Comanche, the Marine Corps developed a program that included four hundred Navajo (Dineh) code talkers. They developed and used a special military dictionary using Navajo words for battle directions and machinery.

Political Movements

United States Marine Private First Class Cecil G. Trosip was a "code talker" during World War II.

The RELOCATION of NATIVE PEOPLES of NORTH AMERICA

Indian men joined some branch of the armed services.[5] Many others worked in war industries and volunteer programs. Again, war bonds were purchased by more Indian people per amount of income than any other American group.

Mainstream as a Threat to Cultural Identity

Unfortunately, the respect for individual Indians who fought in World War II did not extend to respect for Indian culture and life. This was hurtful and frustrating to Indians returning from fighting valiantly in the American cause. John Collier's dream of a multicultural society in which many races, religions, and cultures could live side by side, was overwhelmed by the common wish that everyone be the same. And that "same" was mainstream white America. The 1950s was a particularly difficult time for diversity, as the Cold War and the fear of different types of government caused suspicion and intolerance against many groups of people. Some Americans even thought that tribalism was similar to Communism.

Assimilation—Indians being absorbed into white society without recognition of their own culture—became the governmental goal. A 1946 Indian Claims Commission, formed to clear up any disputed treaty claims, was coupled with yet another relocation policy. This one, instead of the infamous Trail of Tears leading toward future reservations, was formed to *dissolve* those reservations and send Indians off to cities. This proposed termination of reservations completely contradicted the idea of an Indian cultural revival.

Political Movements

Land Claims in Canada

Since the 1970s a number of court cases and negotiations between Aboriginal groups and the government have dealt with claims in regard to obligations under historic treaties. Between 1973 and 2014, twenty-six modern treaties have been concluded. These agreements, known as Comprehensive Claims, have provided First Nations ownership of over 600,000 square kilometers (about 232,000 square miles) as well as the associated self-government rights.

One of the most important agreements was the Nunavut Land Claims Agreement signed in 1993, which led to the creation of the Territory of Nunavut out of the eastern portion of the Northwest Territories six years later, which encompasses the traditional lands of the Inuit.[6]

Prejudice and Poverty

Many reservations had again become pockets of poverty during the time that so many energetic young Indian people were involved in World War II. It was confusing to have been in France and Germany with army wages and come home to a reservation that was rural, had no jobs to offer, and held many people,

The RELOCATION of NATIVE PEOPLES of NORTH AMERICA

Prejudice against American Indians continued into the 1940s and 1950s. This sign was posted behind a bar in Montana.

old and young, who felt confused and discouraged. Offered job training by the government, a one-way ticket, a shoddy apartment, and an alarm clock—so they could get up on time to go to work—many native people left the reservations for cities.

When they had to compete for jobs in an urban setting, Indians encountered prejudice and discrimination. They often became just as poor and discouraged as they had been at home on the reservation. Only now, they were isolated culturally as well. There was, for many, a gradual return to the reservation, where at least family could be counted on to help.

Herding wide-ranging, well-organized tribes onto small portions of their land caused terrible misery.

Political Movements

Ironically, after World War II, the termination of reservations threatened to bring about what many people thought was inevitable in the nineteenth century: the possible extinction of American Indian culture.

The termination policy was legally passed in 1953. Each state was to deal with this law. When it was completely implemented, Indians would cease to exist as an entity to be dealt with separately by the government. There would be no more governmental responsibility toward American Indians.

Termination was not about freedom, it was about the government no longer being responsible for the tribes they had put on the reservations in the first place. What Indians wanted was to be recognized as Indians with tribal identification as well as American citizenship. The NCAI helped them speak up against termination. By the late 1940s, Indians had fought for America in two world wars. Some had college degrees, and the reforms of the IRA and the Indian New Deal had brought them legal and political skills. Congress agreed, in 1958, to only terminate a tribe if the termination was voluntary. By this time, organized, skilled opposition from tribal representatives had begun to have an effect.

Alaska became a state in 1959. The state was offered 103 million acres of federal land that could be developed commercially. This would help the state become economically successful. As in past land-grabs all over the United States, the government did not bother to consult, or even learn about how Alaskan Indians used the lands in question. Because

124 The RELOCATION of NATIVE PEOPLES of NORTH AMERICA

A map shows Alaska's federal lands and reservations. Alaska natives were granted forty-four million acres of land under the Alaska Native Claims Settlement A(ct) (ANSCA) of 1971.

FEDERAL LANDS AND INDIAN RESERVATIONS

- Bureau of Indian Affairs
- Bureau of Land Management / Wilderness
- Department of Defense (includes Army Corps of Engineers lakes)
- Fish and Wildlife Service / Wilderness
- Forest Service / Wilderness
- National Park Service / Wilderness

Political Movements

of the highly organized work of the Alaska Federation of Natives (AFN), in 1966 a freeze was placed on land selection—including the Trans-Alaska pipeline construction. By 1971 the Alaska Native Claims Settlement Act (ANCSA) was passed. "Under ANSCA, native people were given 962 million dollars and forty-four million acres of land," says historian Philip Deloria. Eighty thousand Alaska natives with very different interests and work lives had banded together to make this possible. However, even this landmark legislation was controversial because it was based on American political and business structures.[7]

Indian Advocacy

In the rest of the country, the New Frontier, Great Society, and War on Poverty programs helped Indians join the political struggle for employment, legal solutions to problems on the reservations, and better management of funds and resources. But often political freedom is not without political struggle. The 1960s and early 1970s were a time of rebellion against social and gender inequalities. This became known as "identity politics," and for some American Indians it meant a return to tribal rituals and practices of the past. The National Indian Youth Council (NIYC) of 1961 and the American Indian Movement (AIM), started in the mid-1960s, staged public events to air their grievances against the government.

Two early protests were the sit-in at the deserted prison Alcatraz Island, and the Trail of Broken Treaties march to BIA headquarters. However, the

Pressured Into Poverty

The Menominee are American Indians in Wisconsin who were running a thriving lumber and sawmill business on their reservation in the 1940s. Though there was no good reason for this successful reservation to be terminated, the government pressured the Menominee to do so. They were offered money to compensate for US Forest Service mismanagement—7.6 million dollars. But that money would only be given to them if they agreed to terminate the reservation and become a county. Then, all sorts of new government regulations were insisted upon.

The Menominee fought this termination from 1947 to 1961. When the whole tribe had sunk into poverty because of corrupt white control, they struggled to regain their federal trust position. The same thing happened to the Klamath, living on a 1.3 million-acre reservation. They were prosperous on land that was coveted for timber and ranching. But after agreeing to termination, the Klamath fell into chronic poverty.

Political Movements

A group of American Indians occupy the former prison at Alcatraz Island. They stand under graffiti welcoming Indian occupiers to "United Indian property" on the dock of Alcatraz Island.

protest most Americans remember occurred at Wounded Knee. Revisiting the scene of the massacre at Wounded Knee, South Dakota, activists from AIM and the Oglala Lakota Sioux, who lived on the Pine Ridge reservation, occupied the town. A battle began between government forces and the Indians.

Much more than being a standoff between the government and Indians, Wounded Knee of 1973 represented a conflict "between Indian people who

The RELOCATION of NATIVE PEOPLES of NORTH AMERICA

believed in working 'outside the system' and those who found success working within it," says Phillip Deloria.[8] The major achievement of the AIM movement was a document called *The Twenty Points*, which asked for recognition of old treaty promises.

After the Wounded Knee standoff of 1973, Indian activists were persecuted on many fronts. However, the horror over what had happened at Wounded Knee actually sparked increased federal funds and pro-Indian legislation which lasted until the mid-1980s. But then, large-scale social service underfunding again found tribes so impoverished that they were tempted to sell their remaining land. Religious freedom was again a government target, and federal programs and legal rights were slashed.

Conditions on reservations varied. The Pine Ridge reservation, according to national statistics on poverty, was declared the poorest county in the United States. Unemployment rates for most reservations were very high. The side effects of poverty and unemployment are crime, domestic abuse, diabetes, and depression. Alcoholism was a particular problem, and long, straight roads in sparsely populated areas are often lined with white crosses symbolizing Indians who died in auto accidents while intoxicated. The incidence of babies born with fetal alcohol syndrome due to a mother's alcohol consumption increased, as did the threat of AIDS. Suicide rates were high. Indian reservations had the worst health care in the country.

There are, however, stories about successful adaptation. "The BIA," says George Russell, "is not

Political Movements

In 1980 Kickapoo Indians gather around a spigot in their village near the border town of Eagle Pass, Texas.

the enemy. In fairness to the BIA today, it should be understood that, in 176 years, many past sins and much of the chaos was institutionalized and inherited. I personally know and have worked with BIA personnel over the years who are capable and dedicated."[9]

Chapter 12

Reservations Today

Today, almost fifty-six million acres of reservation land are held in trust by the federal government and reserved for American Indians. Nearly half of the reservation population is non-Indian (46 percent) and eleven million acres of land within reservations is owned by non-Indians (20 percent). This came about largely through long-term effects of the Dawes Act.[1]

The Biggest Reservation

The Navajo Nation encompasses the largest geographical territory of any reservation—seventeen million acres in four states, with 110 community chapters. The Navajo have a history of adapting in order to survive. No alcohol is allowed on reservation territory, and tourist trips through historic land such as Canyon De Chelly must be led by a Navajo guide. Navajo weavers and silversmiths have made a name for themselves worldwide, and the Navajo customs and

Political Movements

Navajo weaver Lillie Taylor sells her work at a booth at the Santa Fe Indian market.

The RELOCATION of NATIVE PEOPLES of NORTH AMERICA

religious ceremonies are still practiced throughout the beautiful but largely nonagricultural land of the reservation.

Life on Present-Day Reservations

Reservations do not look like they did in the mid- and late-nineteenth century. With some exceptions, they hold towns with stores and streets of houses, schools, and other public buildings. The most notable exception to this is the Hopi reservation town on top of Hopi mesa in Arizona. There the inhabitants live in pueblo-style houses that take a visitor back to the days before Columbus.

At the Taos Pueblo in New Mexico, the traditional pueblo housing is constantly refurbished and improved, though there is still no electricity or running water. The Navajo reservation still has a few traditional dwellings called hogans.

Many reservations hold ceremonies, some open to the public, that recreate the rituals and dances of the past. The Assiniboine reservation in northeast Montana still has the frames of sweat lodges along the Missouri river. These are used actively by tribal members, whose daily lives are the same as non-Indians in terms of work and school. Most reservations are still well below the national average in poverty and health statistics. The level of organization in the tribal government varies widely from reservation to reservation.

Reservations Today

Traditional pueblo housing is still used in Taos, New Mexico.

Crisis on Canadian Reserves

Although steps have been taken to improve the economic situation and the social well-being of indigenous people living on reserves in Canada, the conditions are often not nearly as good as in the rest of the country. The rates of unemployment and poverty are high, housing poor, substance abuse and suicides frighteningly common. James Anaya, Special Rapporteur on the rights of indigenous peoples for the United Nations, stated in his 2014 report that "Canada faces a continuing crisis when it comes to the situation of indigenous peoples of the country."[2]

First Nations are tackling these challenges in different ways. The remote Ontario reserve of the Kitchenuhmaykoosib Inninuwug offers Canadians the opportunity to visit for a week. By giving tourists an

The RELOCATION of NATIVE PEOPLES of NORTH AMERICA

Legal Definitions of Tribes and Bands

What is an American Indian tribe today? The legal definition is

> Any Indian tribe, band, nation, rancheria, pueblo, colony or community which is recognized by the United States government as eligible for programs and services provided by the Secretary of the Interior to Indians because of their status as Indians.[3]

Similarly, the Canadian Indian Act defines a band as

> a body of Indians
>
> (a) for whose use and benefit in common, lands, the legal title to which is vested in Her Majesty, have been set apart before, on or after September 4, 1951;
>
> (b) for whose use and benefit in common, moneys are held by Her Majesty; or
>
> (c) declared by the Governor in Council to be a band for the purposes of this Act.[4]

Reservations Today

A First Nations member stands on land in British Columbia that was taken from his tribe.

insight into the good and bad of their lives the locals hope to raise awareness of their living conditions and to fight racism.[5]

By contrast, Yellow Quill First Nation has secured reserve status for a property in downtown Saskatoon. The plan is to build an office complex on this land formerly used as a parking lot so that the money earned through renting offices can be reinvested into the First Nation community.[6]

Restoring Nature

Recently, the Cocopah Indians south of Yuma, Arizona, have started a restoration project on the Colorado River. This is an excellent example of cooperation between private and governmental agencies and the leadership of a small tribe. The Cocopah reservation was established in 1917 and made larger in 1985. It is divided into three separate parts and as little as twenty years ago held five thousand Cocopah Indians. Now the population has sunk to eight hundred. The Colorado River that ran through the reservation began to slowly drain away because of the dam upriver. Many fish species became extinct. This affected not only the Cocopah themselves who fished the river, but an ecotourism fishing industry the Cocopah were hoping would help them financially.

With grants from the BIA, the Environmental Protection Agency, the Bureau of Land Management, and the National Wildlife Federation, restoration projects are under way. These include removal of invasive salt cedar trees that choked out the native

Reservations Today

A young Native American girl performs the Butterfly Dance at a rodeo in Cheyenne, Wyoming.

plants that allowed a large population of birds to thrive. Negotiations continue to allow more water to be diverted back along the stretch of the Colorado River that is on the reservation. Says tribal elder Colin Soto: "The thing that ties me back to history is the river. If we restore it, we will be able to not only have some rejuvenation of our culture but be able to take people from town and the schools and say, 'This is who I am. This is Cocopah.'"[7]

Similar conservation projects are under way on the Ute reservation in Colorado and the Walker River Paiute reservation. The devastating effects on water safety of wholesale strip mining on the one remaining official reservation in Oklahoma show up in birth defects and increased cancer rates.[8]

Gambling as a Source of Income

The industry that has gotten the most media attention for the reservations is the gaming industry—the establishment of casinos for legalized gambling. Because reservations are sovereign nations, they do not have to obey the same laws, in most instances, as other states. The reservations are also exempt from taxes, so the casinos can generate a great deal of tax-free income for a tribe. The largest casino has been built by the Mashantucket Pequot of Connecticut, a very small remnant of the powerful Pequot confederacy nearly exterminated in the seventeenth century by settlers.

Only 13 percent of Indian nations have gaming and only five or six reservations are generating

Reservations Today

Mohegan Sun is a casino in Connecticut that is owned and operated by the Mohegan tribe.

wealth. However, for those tribes, the prosperity that should be all positive has drawbacks. The sudden presence of the casino, tourists, and wealth in formerly poor communities has been disruptive. How do you retain cultural values in the face of the total materialism represented by casino gambling, originally a non-Indian development? On the Mohawk reservation, the conflict between different factions, and the gulf between rich and poor, actually led to armed conflict among tribal members.

This conflict between the new prosperity and traditional values worries some who believe casino gambling may not be good for the tribe in the long run. Historian James Wilson points out:

The RELOCATION of NATIVE PEOPLES of NORTH AMERICA

Native Americans, they know, are trapped in a perennial Catch-22: if they appear to live up to their stereotype as "poor," "lazy," and "dependent on welfare" they are seen as a drain on the hard-working American taxpayer and provoke calls for the government to stop featherbedding [taking full care of] them; if, on the other hand, they show some initiative and visibly prosper—as the experience of the Five Civilized Tribes [the Cherokee, Chickasaw, Choctaw, Creek, and Seminole nations] and the terminated peoples like the Menominee testify—outraged citizens promptly demand that their reservations should be dissolved and they should be "treated just like anyone else."[9]

Identity Crisis

The Passamaquoddy of Maine won a substantial court victory in 1980, which confirmed their recognition as a tribe and entitled them to federal services, land, and good schools. However, these good schools rarely spend much time teaching the native language and often alienate students from their parents. Says Wayne Newell, a tribal member who works in a large Passamaquoddy school, "To witness the dying of your language on a daily basis is a really painful experience . . . It's really painful. And I don't think it's possible for people to really understand unless they're in this predicament."[10] This leads into what is one of the largest issue facing Native Americans today: the question of identity.

Because of the dislocations, the uprooting of Aboriginal societies, and the intermarriage with people of other American Indian groups and whites,

Reservations Today

being an Indian is not just a tribal affiliation. Saginaw-Chippewa historian George Russell speaks of this as racially hyphenated Indians. Who is Indian, "either by legal definition or by self-identification, has become an important issue for Indians and their respective tribes."[11]

In the 2010 Census, 5.2 million people identified as American Indian and Alaska Native, 2.3 million of whom specified that they were Indian in combination with one or more additional races.[12] However, 22 percent of those Indians live in American Indian and Alaska Native areas, while 78 percent live elsewhere. In addition, it is estimated that some fifteen million people "believe they have an Indian ancestor but have lost their tribal connection," says Russell.[13]

In Canada, nearly half of the people with Registered Indian status live on reserves, while 50.7% live elsewhere. However, a quarter of the First Nations population are not Registered Indians.[14]

These figures reveal three critical problems facing today's Indian population. One of these is blood quantum. This means not only how much Indian versus non-Indian blood a person might have, but how much of which tribal blood an Indian has. For instance, even if an Indian were full-blood, points out historian Russell, "if a Navajo man marries a Hopi woman; and their Navajo-Hopi son marries a Sioux-Crow wife; and their Navajo-Hopi-Sioux Crow grandson marries a Pima-Kaw-Apache-Ute wife; their great-grandchildren are Navajo-Hopi-Sioux-Crow-Pima-Kaw-Apache-Ute."[15]

142 The RELOCATION of NATIVE PEOPLES of NORTH AMERICA

A Navajo mother and daughter outside a traditional hogan. With each new generation, more Indians are marrying outside of their tribe and the number of full-blooded Indians is decreasing.

Reservations Today

In just four generations, these grandchildren, though full-blooded Indians, have one-eighth blood quantum from eight different tribes. Most tribes have a one-quarter blood quantum minimum for membership. Therefore, these grandchildren cannot be members of any of their tribes. Without an enrolled tribal membership, Indians are not eligible

By the Numbers

In the United States, there are 566 federally recognized American Indian tribes, 229 of which are in Alaska. An additional 64 tribes are state-recognized. In the 2010 census, 5.2 million people (1.7 percent of the total population) identified as American Indian or Alaska Native, and the size of tribes ranged from several in California with only two or three members to the Navajo Nation with 332,129 members and the Cherokee Nation with 819,105 members.[16]

In Canada, 4.3 percent of the population had an Aboriginal identity in 2011. Roughly 850,000 people identified as belonging to one of the more than 600 First Nations/Indian bands, 450,000 identified as Métis, and 60,000 identified as Inuit.[17]

The RELOCATION of NATIVE PEOPLES of NORTH AMERICA

Many festivals celebrating Indian art are now held throughout America and Canada. Tony Abeyta is a Navajo painter whose work is displayed at the Native Treasures Indian Arts Festival in Santa Fe, New Mexico.

for federal programs. Says Russell, "The bottom line is that theoretically, the Indian gene pool will become smaller with each generation until it is extinguished."[18]

Another problem raised by these census statistics is how to continue connections between off-reservation, or urban, American Indians and Indians on the reservation. The loss of tribal language is an obvious outgrowth of these issues. Of the five hundred distinct Indian languages spoken in 1492, 350 have already become extinct and 150 are endangered. Predictions from linguists are that by 2050, only twenty Indian languages will remain.[19]

Reservations Today

Despite these discouraging statistics, a cultural renaissance is taking place within Indian communities and as a result art and environmentalism are flowering. This has led to interest by non-Indians who appreciate Indian art and the ways Indians interacted with the environment.

However, this has not changed the difficulties facing Indian people today. Many economic initiatives are being formed, with current support from federal and private conservation groups helping them succeed. And yet, the constantly shifting land areas and population groups on reservations, the rate of intermarriage and the still alarming health, education, and employment statistics, pose problems for the future. George Russell places hope for future generations in the hands of his own people:

> American Indian destiny is at a crossroads. Indians must prepare to take control of their destiny, as gently as possible. The next battles will be won by attorneys whose weapons are the legal briefs and laptop computers... American Indians have the responsibility, to those ancestors who fired arrows against cannons and survived against overwhelming odds, to make that survival meaningful.[20]

TIMELINE

1492   Columbus arrives in the New World and thinks he has reached the East Indies. He calls the native population "Indians."

1539   Hernando de Soto reaches the Southeast. He systematically slaughters the inhabitants and spreads disease.

1605   Port-Royal, the first French settlement in North America, is founded.

1607   Jamestown colony is founded by a group of English settlers.

1620   Plymouth colony is founded by a group of English colonists; many of them seek freedom to worship as they choose.

1744   Treaty of Lancaster is signed.

1755   The British administration creates the Indian Department.

1763   The Royal Proclamation regulating the relations of the British Crown with North American Aboriginals is issued.

1775   American Revolution begins with most Indian tribes on the British side.

1776   Declaration of Independence is signed and distributed.

1778   First treaty between Indians and the new United States government.

1783   American Revolution ends, with negative results for Indian independence.

1803   Louisiana Purchase opens up the West; Lewis and Clark prepare to explore.

1824   Bureau of Indian Affairs (BIA) is established.

1830   Indian Removal Act is passed. This leads to thousands of families being marched to Indian Territory. Many die along the "Trail of Tears."

1848   Gold is discovered in California and miners and settlers pour into American Indian lands.

1850   United States legislation stops all foreign land claims.

Timeline

1854	Indian Appropriation Act legalizes the reservations that the territories had established for Indians during the implementation of the Removal Act of 1830.
1861-1865	Civil War is fought. Many tribes are forced to take sides and funds for reservations are even scarcer.
1864	The Navajo Long Walk begins.
1868	Fort Laramie peace conference is held. Ten Sioux tribes and the Arapahoe sign treaties.
1870	Ghost Dance religion begins, drawing many tribes into a hope for spiritual renewal.
1871	End of treaties between United States and Indians.
1876	Defeat of General Custer at the Little Big Horn in Montana by Sioux and Cheyenne warriors. Canada's Indian Act is passed.
1879	Carlisle Indian School, in Pennsylvania, is founded.
1887	Dawes Act subdivides American Indian lands into single-family acreage.
1890	The Battle of Wounded Knee occurs. American troops massacre more than three hundred Sioux and Cheyenne men, women, and children.
1895	Only a thousand buffalo are left on the plains; American Indians are forced to move to reservations to avoid starvation.
1917-1918	United States enters World War I; American Indian soldiers distinguish themselves in battle.
1924	American Indians become United States citizens.
1934	Indian Reorganization Act ends allotment but severe checkerboarding of reservation land creates confusion and more poverty.
1941-1945	United States enters World War II; Navajo code talkers are used extensively.
1944	National Congress of American Indians is created.

The RELOCATION of NATIVE PEOPLES of NORTH AMERICA

1946	Indian Claims Commission Act, originally established to help Indians settle claims against the US government, leads to BIA efforts at relocation.
1954	Termination and Relocation Act sends seventeen thousand Indians from the reservations to the cities.
1960	Aboriginals in Canada receive the right to vote in federal elections.
1973	Returning from a march on Washington, D.C., to protest "Trail of Broken Treaties," Indians take over the town of Wounded Knee.
1975	Indian Self-Determination and Education Assistance Act.
1978	American Indian Religious Freedom Act and the Indian Child Welfare Act.
1985	By introducing Bill C-31, discriminatory elements are taken out of Canada's Indian Act.
1988	Indian Gaming Regulatory Act allows several tribes to start gambling casinos on their reservations.
1989	Smithsonian Institution consolidates Indian collections.
1994	The Smithsonian's National Museum of the American Indian (NMAI) facility opens in New York City.
1999	Another NMAI facility opens in Suitland, Maryland. Nunavut, Canada's newest territory that encompasses the traditional lands of the Inuit, is created by being officially separated from the Northwest Territories.
2004	NMAI's main facility and museum opens on the National Mall in Washington, D.C.
2013	US Congress passes law allowing Indian tribes to prosecute non-Indians in cases of domestic violence on Indian land.

CHAPTER NOTES

Chapter 1. Resistance Against Reservations
1. Debra Buchholtz, *The Battle of the Greasy Grass/Little Bighorn: Custer's Last Stand in Memory, History, and Popular Culture* (New York: Routledge, 2012), 185.
2. John Keegan, *Fields of Battle: The Wars for North America* (New York: Albert A. Knopf, 1996), 287.

Chapter 2. The Coming of the Europeans
1. Charles C. Mann, *1491, New Revelations of the Americas Before Columbus* (New York: Alfred A. Knopf, 2005), 94.
2. George Russell, *American Indian Facts of Life* (Phoenix, Ariz.: Russell Publications, 2004), 25.
3. Mann, 105.
4. Statistics Canada, "Introduction to Censuses of Canada, 1665 to 1871," accessed February 27, 2015, http://www.statcan.gc.ca/pub/98-187-x/2000001/4198819-eng.pdf.
5. Francis Paul Prucha, *Atlas of American Indian Affairs* (Lincoln, Neb.: University of Nebraska Press, 1990), 142.
6. Ralph K. Andrist, in Clark Wissler, *Red Man Reservations* (New York: Collier Books, 1971), ix.
7. Russell Thornton, *American Indian Holocaust and Survival: A Population History Since 1492* (Norman, Okla.: University of Oklahoma Press, 1987), 35.

Chapter 3. The Loss of Freedom
1. George Russell, *American Indian Facts of Life* (Phoenix, Ariz.: Native Data Network, 2004), 26.
2. Volker Depkat, *Geschichte Nordamerikas: Eine Einführung* (Cologne, Germany: Böhlau Verlag, 2008), 203–204.
3. Landon Y. Jones, *William Clark and the Shaping of the West* (New York: Hill and Wang, 2004), 21.
4. Alan Taylor, *The Divided Ground* (New York: Alfred A. Knopf, 2006), 32.
5. James Wilson, *The Earth Shall Weep* (New York: Grove Press, 1998), 127.
6. Jones, 22.
7. Jones, 85.

8. Richard White, in Betty Ballantine and Ian Ballantine, eds., *The Native Americans: An Illustrated History* (North Dighton, Mass.: World Publications Group, 2001), 293.

Chapter 4. Supplanting the Natives

1. Klaus Frantz, *Indian Reservations in the United States* (Chicago: University of Chicago Press, 1999), 13.
2. Landon Y. Jones, *William Clark and the Shaping of the West* (New York: Hill and Wang, 2004), 279–280.
3. George Russell, *American Indian Facts of Life* (Phoenix, Ariz.: Native Data Network, 2004), 51.
4. Ibid.
5. Ibid.
6. Ibid., 77.
7. Jones, 292.
8. Ibid., 293.
9. Peter Nabokov, in Betty Ballantine and Ian Ballantine, eds., *The Native Americans: An Illustrated History* (North Dighton, Mass.: World Publications Group, 2001), 309.

Chapter 5. Pushing Westward and Northward

1. Landon Y. Jones, *William Clark and the Shaping of the West* (New York: Hill and Wang, 2004), 331.
2. Ibid.
3. Jones, 331.
4. Peter Nabokov, in Betty Ballantine and Ian Ballantine, eds., *The Native Americans: An Illustrated History* (North Dighton, Mass.: World Publications Group, 2001), 312.
5. Ibid., 321.
6. David B. Guralink, ed., *Webster's New World Dictionary* (New York: Simon and Schuster, 1980), 1208.
7. Catherine Soames, ed., *The Oxford Compact English Dictionary* (Oxford: Oxford University Press, 2003), 968.
8. Government of Canada Justice Laws Web site, "Indian Act," accessed February 27, 2015, http://laws-lois.justice.gc.ca/eng/acts/I-5/FullText.html.
9. Aboriginal Affairs and Northern Development Canada. "First Nations in Canada," accessed February 27. 2015, https://www.aadnc-aandc.gc.ca/DAM/DAM-INTER-HQ-AP/STAGING/texte-text/fnc_1382036254169_eng.epub.

Chapter Notes

10. James Wilson, *The Earth Shall Weep* (New York: Grove Press, 1998), 267.
11. Ibid., 270.
12. Ibid., 271.

Chapter 6. Armed Conflict

1. Dee Alexander Brown, *Bury My Heart at Wounded Knee: An Indian History of the American West* (New York: Sterling, 2009), 143.
2. William Brandon, *The American Heritage Book of Indians* (New York: Dell Publishing Company, 1971), 352.
3. James Wilson, *The Earth Shall Weep* (New York: Grove Press, 1998), 269.
4. The Council on Interracial Books for Children, ed., *Chronicles of American Indian Protest* (New York: Fawcett Books,1971), 235.
5. Peter Nabokov, in Betty Ballantine and Ian Ballantine, eds., *The Native Americans: An Illustrated History* (North Dighton, Mass.: World Publications Group, 2001), 316.
6. Wilson, 280–281.
7. Nabokov, 330.
8. Ibid.
9. Ibid.
10. George F. Stanley, "Louis Riel," *The Canadian Encyclopedia*. accessed February 27, 2015, http://www.thecanadianencyclopedia.ca/en/article/louis-riel/.
11. Nabokov, 339.
12. George Russell, *American Indian Facts of Life* (Phoenix, Ariz.: Native Data Network, 2004), 34.
13. Wilson, p. 153.

Chapter 7. Indian Suffering

1. Peter Nabokov, in Betty Ballantine and Ian Ballantine, eds., *The Native Americans: An Illustrated History* (North Dighton, Mass.: World Publications Group, 2001), 364.
2. Ibid., 365.
3. James Wilson, *The Earth Shall Weep* (New York: Grove Press, 1998), 285.
4. Dee Brown, *Bury My Heart at Wounded Knee* (New York: Holt, Rinehart & Winston, New York, 1970), 444.
5. Nabokov, 366.

6. George Russell, *American Indian Facts of Life* (Phoenix, Ariz.: Native Data Network, 2004), 87.
7. Wilson, 305.
8. Nabokov, 369.
9. Wilson, 309.
10. Indigenous Foundations, "The Indian Act," accessed February 27, 2015, http://indigenousfoundations.arts.ubc.ca/home/government-policy/the-indian-act.html.
11. Jay Makarenko, "The Indian Act: Historical Overview," *Maple Leaf Web*, 2008, accessed February 27, 2015, http://mapleleafweb.com/features/the-indian-act-historical-overview.

Chapter 8. Forced Assimilation

1. James Wilson, *The Earth Shall Weep* (New York: Grove Press, 1998), 312.
2. Ibid., 315.
3. J. R. Miller, "Residential Schools," *The Canadian Encyclopedia*, accessed February 27, 2015, http://www.thecanadianencyclopedia.ca/en/article/residential-schools/.
4. George Russell, *American Indian Facts of Life* (Phoenix, Ariz.: Native Data Network, 2004).
5. Peter Nabokov, in Betty Ballantine and Ian Ballantine, eds., *The Native Americans: An Illustrated History* (North Dighton, Mass.: World Publications Group, 2001), 368.
6. Ibid., 341.
7. Ibid., 343.
8. Clark Wissler, *Red Man Reservations* (New York: Collier Books, 1971), 64.
9. Ibid.
10. Ibid., 65.
11. Ibid.

Chapter 9. Buyout of Indian Land

1. Peter Nabokov, in Betty Ballantine and Ian Ballantine, eds., *The Native Americans: An Illustrated History* (North Dighton, Mass.: World Publications Group, 2001), 373.
2. Ibid., 374.
3. Ibid., 369.
4. Ibid., 374.
5. Ibid., 379.
6. James Wilson, *The Earth Shall Weep* (New York: Grove Press, 1998), 245.

Chapter Notes

Chapter 10. Steps Toward Multiculturalism

1. James Wilson, *The Earth Shall Weep* (New York: Grove Press, 1998), 348.
2. George Russell, *American Indian Facts of Life* (Phoenix, Ariz.: Native Data Network, 2004), 73.
3. Aboriginal Affairs and Northern Development Canada, "First Nations in Canada," accessed February 27, 2015, https://www.aadnc-aandc.gc.ca/DAM/DAM-INTER-HQ-AP/STAGING/texte-text/fnc_1382036254169_eng.epub.
4. Wilson, 357.
5. Philip J. Deloria, in Betty Ballantine and Ian Ballantine, eds., *The Native Americans: An Illustrated History* (North Dighton, Mass.: World Publications, 2001), 388.
6. Ibid., 403.

Chapter 11. Political Movements

1. Michael E. Marchand. *The River of Life: Sustainable Practices of Native Americans and Indigenuous Peoples* (Boston and Berlin: Higher Education Press and Walter de Gruyter GmbH, 2014), 134.
2. Philip J. Deloria, in Betty Ballantine and Ian Ballantine, eds., *The Native Americans: An Illustrated History* (North Dighton, Mass.: World Publications Group, 2001), 416.
3. Ibid.
4. Ibid., 423.
5. Ibid., 422.
6. Aboriginal Affairs and Northern Development Canada, "Comprehensive Claims," accessed February 27, 2015, https://www.aadnc-aandc.gc.ca/eng/1100100030577/1100100030578.
7. Deloria, 433.
8. Ibid., 441.
9. George Russell, *American Indian Facts of Life* (Phoenix, Ariz.: Native Data Network, 2004), 89.

Chapter 12. Reservations Today

1. George Russell, *American Indian Facts of Life* (Phoenix, Ariz.: Native Data Network, 2004), 89.
2. James Anaya, "The Situation of Indigenous Peoples in Canada," accessed March 12, 2015, http://unsr.jamesanaya.org/docs/countries/2014-report-canada-a-hrc-27-52-add-2-en.pdf, 20.

The RELOCATION of NATIVE PEOPLES of NORTH AMERICA

3. Russell, 55–56.
4. "Indian Act," Government of Canada Justice Laws, accessed February 27, 2015, http://laws-lois.justice.gc.ca/eng/acts/I-5/FullText.html.
5. Louise Brown, "Northern Reserve 'KI' Wants 25 Ordinary Canadians to Visit to Experience Its Culture," *The Toronto Star*, May 19, 2013, http://www.thestar.com/news/canada/2013/05/19/northern_reserve_ki_wants_25_ordinary_canadians_to_visit_to_experience_its_culture.html.
6. Aaron Streck and Thomas Piller, "First Nation to Build on Urban Reserve in Downtown Saskatoon," Globalnews.ca, October 16, 2014, http://globalnews.ca/news/1616821/first-nation-committed-to-office-complex-in-downtown-saskatoon/.
7. Jim Morrison, "Emergency Aid for An Ailing River," *National Wildlife Federation Magazine* 44, no. 3 (2006): 13–14.
8. Winona La Duke, "Indigenous Environmental Perspectives," *A North American Primer,* in *Akwekon Journal* 9, no. 2 (1992): 61.
9. James Wilson, *The Earth Shall Weep* (New York: Grove Press, 1998), 417–418.
10. Ibid., 421.
11. Russell, 52.
12. Tina Norris, Paula L. Vines, and Elizabeth M. Hoeffel, "The American Indian and Alaska Native Population: 2010," United States Census Bureau, 2012, http://www.census.gov/prod/cen2010/briefs/c2010br-10.pdf, 7.
13. Russell, 56.
14. Norris, Vines, and Hoeffel, 10–11.
15. Russell, 61.
16. Norris, Vines, and Hoeffel, 17.
17. Statistics Canada, "Aboriginal Peoples in Canada: First Nations People, Métis and Inuit," accessed February 27. 2015, http://www12.statcan.gc.ca/nhs-enm/2011/as-sa/99-011-x/99-011-x2011001-eng.cfm.
18. Russell, 62.
19. Ibid., 65.
20. Statistics Canada, pp. 115, 143.

GLOSSARY

alliance—A close association for similar goals, often of nations or political parties.

allotment—A share or portion. Indian reservations were subdivided into portions with a certain number of acres, one portion per family.

code talker—A person who encoded and deciphered messages in a Native American language for the US Army as a form of secret military code during World War I and II.

ecology—The branch of biology that deals with the relations between all living creatures and their environment.

massacre—The killing of large numbers of people.

pandemic—An epidemic that spreads over a large area.

paradox—A statement of condition that seems to be just the opposite of what it says or does but which may in fact be true.

retaliate—To react to an injury or wrong in the same way it was given.

revitalization—Bringing back energy or spirit after a decline.

spiritual—Having to do with the mind and not the body or material things. For American Indians, it was a tribal and personal connection with nature and land and animals, and of life all around them.

tipi—A cone-shaped tent of animal skins used by the Plains Indians.

trance—A state of changed consciousness, somewhat like sleep. American Indians use trances to reach and express spiritual connection.

treaty—A document representing a formal agreement or contract between two or more nations. Usually this refers to trade, peace, or an alliance.

FURTHER READING

Books

Gagne, Tammy. *Life on the Reservations.* Hockessin, Del.: Mitchell Lane Publishers, 2014.

Greenhaven Press. *Native Americans.* San Diego: Greenhaven Press, 2012.

Kuiper, Kathleen. *Indigenous Peoples of the Arctic, Subarctic, and Northwest Coast.* New York: Rosen, 2011.

McCormick, Anita Louise. *The Native American Struggle in United States History.* Berkeley Heights, N.J.: Enslow, 2015.

Nardo, Don. *The Relocation of the American Indian.* San Diego: ReferencePoint Press, 2014.

Web Sites

aadnc-aandc.gc.ca/
Aboriginal Affairs and Northern Development Canada supports the social and economic well-being of Aboriginal people and Northerners.

canadiana.ca/citm/
The Canada in the Making project explores the history of Canada through primary sources and narratives.

americanindian.si.edu/
The National Museum of the American Indian contains one of the world's largest collections of Native artifacts, with many collections available in an online catalog.

INDEX

A

agency stores, 93
Alaska, 11, 123, 125, 141, 143
Alaska Federation of Natives (AFN), 125
Alaska Native Claims Settlement Act (ANCSA), 125
Alcatraz Island protest, 125, 127
alcohol/alcoholism, 38, 43, 49, 64, 89, 128, 130
Algonquin, 15–16, 18
American Indian Defense Association (AIDA), 106
American Indian Movement (AIM), 125, 128
American Indians. *See also specific tribes.*
   in Civil War, 47–48, 89
   early history, 9–11, 13, 15–17
   education and schools, 56, 81–83, 85, 91, 101, 106, 112, 114, 132, 140, 145
   identity, retention of, 82, 120, 125, 140–141, 143–145
   intermarriage and, 24, 140, 145
   population of, 9–10, 17, 26, 49–50, 63, 71, 104, 130, 136, 141, 143, 145
   poverty and, 75, 89–93, 98, 100, 112, 114, 121–123, 125–126, 128, 132–133
   protests of, 73, 96, 106, 125, 127
   religion and, 64–65, 76, 106, 128, 132
   slavery of, 17, 50
   starvation of, 17, 26, 31, 48, 51, 53, 71, 89, 90–95
   tribes and bands defined, 134, 140–141, 143–144
   wars, and armed conflicts, 19–23, 40, 42–43, 47, 49–63, 64
   in white society, 24, 30–31, 51, 56, 64, 69, 76, 85, 94, 112, 120
Amherst, Jeffrey, 21–23
Apache, 44, 50–51, 58, 60, 141
Arapaho, 39, 42, 58, 65, 91
Arikara, 36–37, 42
Assiniboine, 36–37, 42, 132
Atsina, 42

B

Big Foot, 66–67
Blackfeet, 37–38, 44, 58, 91–92
blood quantum issue, 141, 143
bounties on Indian scalps, 18
Bozeman trail, 56
Britain (England), 20–21, 23
buffalo
   Indian dependence upon, 5, 33, 37–39, 64, 77, 92
   slaughtering of, 49, 77, 87
Bureau of Indian Affairs (BIA), 29, 37
   corruption in, 48, 69, 89–90, 114, 116
   formation, 29–31,
   punishment of Indians by, 65, 73
   reform of, 104–106, 108–112, 114, 128–129, 136, 138
   on single-plot ownership, 69, 71
Bursum Bill, 105–106

C

Calhoun, John C., 29
Camp Grant Massacre, 60
Canada
   Aboriginals, 10, 24, 41, 43, 46, 76–77, 79–81, 85, 110, 121, 143
   Bill C-31, 110
   First Nations, 24, 77, 80, 110, 121, 133, 136, 143
   legal development, and treaties in, 76–77, 79–80, 85–86, 110, 121
   reservations, present day, 133, 136, 141, 143
   White Paper, 110
Carlisle Indian School, 82–83, 85, 112
Carson, Kit, 50–51
Cartier, Jacques, 15
casinos, 138–140

The RELOCATION of NATIVE PEOPLES of NORTH AMERICA

Cayuga, 15, 18–19, 25
checkerboarding, 75, 108
Cherokee
    adaptation, attempts, 30–31
    early history, 13, 15
    land and, 31–34, 71, 73–76
    present day, and, 140, 143
    relocation of, 44, 47, 98
    termination of, 31–34
Cherokee Nation v. *State of Georgia*, 31
Cheyenne
    and the Ghost Dance, 64–65
    intertribal politics, 39–40, 42
    massacres of, 5–6, 58
Chickasaw, 15, 32, 71, 73, 98, 140
Chief Black Kettle, 58
Chief Joseph, 51, 53–54
Chief Red Cloud, 56
Chippewa, 10, 63, 99, 115, 118, 141
Choctaw, 15, 32, 71, 73, 98, 100–101, 118
Choctaw telephone code talkers, 100, 118
cholera, 17
Civil War, 47, 89
Clark, William, 28, 32–34, 37
Cochise, 50
Cocopah, 136, 138
Collier, John, 101, 104–106, 108–109, 111–112, 116, 120
Colorado River restoration, 136, 138
Columbus, Christopher, 9–10, 46, 132
Comanche, 33, 39, 42, 44, 118
Crazy Horse, 5–6, 60, 62
Cree, 36–37
Creek, 13, 15, 71, 73, 98–99, 140
Crow, 42, 118
Custer, George Armstrong, 58, 60

D

Darlington, Brinton, 91
Dawes Act, 67, 73, 75, 88, 96, 98, 104, 108, 130
De Prefontaine, Joseph R., 37
De Soto, Hernando, 13
Delaware, 21–22, 30, 32, 39, 98
discrimination, 56, 85, 112, 122
Dobyns, Henry A., 9

E

eminent domain, 97
environmentalism, 136, 138, 145
European settlement, 9, 11, 13, 15, 17, 18–19, 24, 26, 38, 69, 81, 85, 112

F

Federal Indian Health Program, 101
Fort Gary, 61
Fort Laramie peace conference, 56
Fort Nassau, 15
Fox, 118
French and Indian War, 20

G

Galbraith, Thomas, 48
gambling, 138–140
Ghost Dance religion, 64–65, 73
Gibbon, John, 58
gold, 34, 36, 51, 58, 67
Grant, Ulysses S., 56, 89–91

H

Head, Francis Bond, 43
Harper, Stephen, 85
hogan, 51, 93, 132
Hopi, 106, 132, 141
Hudson Bay Company, 61
Huron, 15, 18–19

I

"identity politics," 125
Indian Act (Canada), 41, 78–80, 110, 134
Indian Appropriations Act of 1851, 34
Indian Appropriations Act of 1854, 43–44
Indian Claims Commission, 120
Indian Emergency Conservation Work (IECW) programs, 116
Indian New Deal, 109, 115–117, 123
Indian Peace Commission, 89–90
Indian Red Cross, 100
Indian Removal Act, 31–32
Indian Reorganization Act (IRA), 108–110, 115
Indian Residential School Settlement Agreement (Canada), 85
Inuit, 46, 77, 121, 143

Index

Iroquois,
    Confederacy, 19, 25, 86
    the Five Nations, 18–19, 38
    French and Indian War, 20
    trading, dependence on, 15

J

Jackson, Andrew, 32
Jamestown colony, 13
Jefferson, Thomas, 28
Joseph Medicine Crow, 118

K

Kansas, 33
Kickapoo, 32, 75
King George III, 23
Kiowa, 33, 39, 42, 44
Klamath, 126

L

Lakota Sioux, 6, 37, 49, 56, 76, 127
land issues
    allotment, 67, 69, 71, 73–74, 76,
        97–99, 108, 110, 130
    Indian ownership, 11, 15–17, 23,
        25–26, 28–48, 49–50, 87–89,
        114, 123, 125
    settlers and, 11, 15–17, 18, 23, 26,
        28, 30, 36–48, 53, 73–76, 105
    single-plot ownership, 69, 71
land "runs," 74
language extinction, 13, 82, 104, 140,
    144
League of the Longhouse, 15
Lewis, Meriweather, 28, 37
Little Big Horn, Battle of the, 60, 87–88
Little Crow, 48
longhouses, 15, 93
Louisiana Purchase, 28–29

M

Mandan, 36–37
Mangas Coloradas, 50
Manitoba Act of 1870, 61
Marshall, John, 32
McKinley, William, 96–97
medicine, differing concepts of, 94–95
Menominee, 126, 140

Meriam Report, 106, 108
Métis, 24, 61, 77, 79–80, 143
Mississippi Mound Civilization, 13
Mohawk, 15, 18–19, 25, 112, 139
multiculturalism, 104–106, 108–112, 114
Muskogee, 15, 30

N

National Congress of American Indians
    (NCAI), 116, 123
National Indian Youth Council (NIYC),
    125
Navajo
    code talkers, 118
    enslavement of, 50
    government reorganization by, 111
    present day, 130, 132, 141, 143
    removal of, 43–44, 47, 50–51
Navajo "Long Walk," 51
Nez Perce, 51, 53
North-West Rebellion of 1885, 61
Nunavut, 121

O

Odawa, 25
Ojibwa, 25
Oklahoma Territory, 73–74, 96–98
Oklahombi, Joseph, 100–101
Ollokut, 53
Oneida, 15, 25, 118
Onondaga, 15, 18–19, 25
Osage, 32, 71, 98
Ottawa, 21

P

Parker, Ely S., 56, 89
Passamaquoddy, 140
Pauite, 64, 138
Pawnee, 33, 39
Peoria, 83
Pequot, 138
Pilcher, Joshua, 137
Pine Ridge reservation, 66, 127–128
Plains Indians, 36, 38–39, 42–44, 82, 87
Plymouth colony, 11, 13, 16
Pontiac's Rebellion, 21–23
Potlatch, 78, 110
Pratt, Richard, 82

The RELOCATION of NATIVE PEOPLES of NORTH AMERICA

Pueblo Indians, 44, 104–106, 111

R

Red Cloud, 56
reservations
    during the Civil War, 47, 49
    defined, 41
    early life on, 39, 44, 47–48, 51, 53, 62, 72, 76, 85–95
    establishment of, 31–34
    health care on, 128, 132, 145
    land, present ownership of, 130, 132, 136, 138–140
    legalization, 43–44
    life, to present day, 116, 120–123, 125, 128, 130–132, 136, 138–141, 143–145
    resistance to, 5–6
    termination policies, 39, 56, 58, 60, 120, 123, 126
    unemployment rates, 128, 133
Revolutionary War, 23, 25
Riel, Louis, 61
Roosevelt, Franklin D., 108
Royal Proclamation of 1763, 23

S

Saginaw, 10, 63, 141
Sand Creek Massacre, 58
Santee Sioux, 48
Sauk, 118
Seminole, 32, 71, 73, 98, 140
Seneca, 15, 18–19, 25
Seward, William, 44, 47
Sequoyah, 98
Shawnee, 21, 26, 32, 39
Shoshone, 39, 42
Sioux
    in the Ghost Dance, 64–65
    intertribal politics, 66–67
    Little Big Horn, Battle of the, 60, 62, 87
    massacres of, 60, 66–67
    relocation of, 5–6, 46–47
Sitting Bull, 6, 60, 65
smallpox, 17, 22, 34, 36–37
Society of American Indians, 101

T

Tecumseh, 26
Tenskawatawa, 26
termination policies, 120, 123, 126
Thorpe, Jim, 112
tipi, 6, 13, 93
trading, 15–16, 18–19, 24, 36, 46, 61, 77, 91, 93–94
Trail of, Broken Treaties protest, 125, 127
Trail of Tears, 31–32, 44, 47, 120
Treaty of Greenville, 25–26
Treaty of Lancaster, 23
tribes and bands, defined, 134
The Twenty Points, 127–128
Tuscarora, 15, 25
Two Moons, 5–6

U

United States
    bounties, on Indian scalps, 18
    treaties, breaking of, as policy, 6, 23, 25–26, 28, 39, 43–44, 51, 62–63, 73–75, 85–86, 98–99
    Western settlement, 23, 36, 53
Utes, 44, 75, 138

W

Wampanoag, 11, 15–16
War of 1812, 26, 28
Wissler, Clark, 91–92, 95
Worcester v. *Georgia*, 32
World War I, 98–102
World War II, 116, 118, 120–121, 123
Wounded Knee
    massacre, 65–67, 69, 73, 127
    protest, 127–128

Y

Yahi Yana, 102
Yakima, 44
Yellow Quill, 136

WITHDRAWN

$24.60   7/19/16.

LONGWOOD PUBLIC LIBRARY
800 Middle Country Road
Middle Island, NY 11953
(631) 924-6400
mylpl.net

LIBRARY HOURS

Monday-Friday	9:30 a.m. - 9:00 p.m.
Saturday	9:30 a.m. - 5:00 p.m.
Sunday (Sept-June)	1:00 p.m. - 5:00 p.m.